Social S

for

Amazing
Kids

Learn How to Make Friends and Keep Them, Identify,
Regulate and Communicate Your Feelings, Set Body
Boundaries, Improve Your Attention Skills, and More.

By Miranda Young

Contents

Introduction

"Children must be taught how to think, not what to think."
~ Margaret Mead, Cultural Anthropologist

If I said you would enjoy playing a board game, such as Scrabble, you wouldn't learn anything from me telling you this. Even if you did like Scrabble, you wouldn't necessarily know why – you would need to think and decide for yourself. However, if I taught you the rules of Scrabble, played the game with you, and asked you to explain what you like and don't like about the game, you would learn several things. You'd be allowed to form your opinion of the game without bias (because I wouldn't tell you if I liked it), and you'd also start developing your thinking skills by weighing the pros and cons.

As the quote above by Mead suggests, you'd start learning how to think, not what to think, and this is vital. Thinking skills are key when you're developing your social skills, and that's what this book is all about.

Have you ever struggled when it comes to:

★ Making friends, especially if you're shy?
★ Others doing things you're uncomfortable with?
★ Arguing or resolving conflict with others?
★ Doing well at school?
★ Being more confident?
★ Communicating with others?
★ Taking care of yourself?

Well, developing your social skills can help with that.

You start to be social even as a baby, from the moment you start to learn to interact, communicate, and talk. *That's right, you've been doing it for a long time already!* Even though you've been developing those skills, you may still have a lot to learn. But this isn't a book that will tell you what to do; this is a book that will guide you, so you can consider the skills you need and create your own path.

You can learn how to behave in the right way, communicate and listen better, set boundaries, take care of yourself, make good decisions, deal with conflict, stay positive, and keep developing and growing as a young person as you head toward your teenage years.

As a mom, I know better than most that my son wanted to be independent at a young age. When I looked into this, I realized independence is a key part of developing social skills — I had to educate him and encourage him in a way that helped him figure out the answers for himself. It was a learning journey for me as a parent, so I've written down everything I know, to help you develop your social skills in a way that's comfortable for you.

Developing social skills made a huge difference in my son's life, for the better, as it helped to build his confidence and resilience. It improved his problem-solving and decision-making skills and ensured he was equipped for the situations he faced throughout this important time in his life.

It's time to be confident and enjoy your life, because your childhood years are so important and should be so much fun. However, that doesn't mean they don't come without their challenges.

But what if you knew exactly what to do and how to navigate your life?

This book will show you how to strengthen your friendships and overcome the challenges you face, while also inspiring you. Imagine being able to manage your emotions, solve your problems, and respect boundaries while setting your own. These aren't skills you'll learn in school, but they'll help you live a happy life. *The life you want!*

Let's start by finding out exactly what social skills are and why they're so important!

Chapter 1:

Why Do I Need Social Skills?

Social skills are a key part of your development throughout your childhood and teenage years. They can help you communicate and engage with other people, but they also ensure you can let others know how you feel, what you want, and if you need anything.

Everyone develops social skills, but the better your skills are, the more likely you are to have a successful and happy life. You're never too young to develop those skills, so the earlier you start, the more you get to practice, and the better you get.

Social skills are complex, so it's important you gain an understanding of what they are and how you can refine them. This chapter will focus on what social skills are, which ones you need, and why they are so important. We'll finish off with a little activity that will help you identify your own strengths in relation to your social skills. Children who develop strong social skills at a young age are more likely to form friendships more easily, which positively impacts their mental health, as they can resolve conflict and problems more efficiently.

Before we go any further, let's clarify exactly what social skills are...

What Are Social Skills?

Social skills are basically a collection of soft skills you need in order to communicate and interact with others in a positive way. You use them daily through speaking, facial expressions, and body language.

They allow you to grow as a person, which is why they are things you need to know about at your age.

But what social skills do you need exactly?

Let's look at social skills in real-life settings and discover which ones you need to develop.

Which Social Skills Do I Need?

At your age, you're starting to develop your own interests and form bonds with your friends, but you're also growing in independence. Sometimes, you may fall out with your friends or feel pressure to do things you don't want to do, but developing your social skills can help you build the confidence to make your own decisions, which includes being comfortable saying no.

In this book, we've put together 16 of the most important social skills you will need, which include:

★ Communicating and listening
★ Managing your emotions
★ Maintaining friendships
★ Cooperation
★ Negotiation
★ Problem-solving
★ Decision-making
★ Reaching your potential
★ Being responsible
★ Improving your attention
★ Engagement
★ Good manners
★ Empathy

- ★ Respecting boundaries
- ★ Positivity
- ★ Kindness

The good news...

All these skills are covered in this book, in 11 easy steps.

Why Are Social Skills So Important?

There are so many benefits to improving your social skills. For example, knowing how to act in difficult situations can reduce your stress and anxiety. They will also help you with your reasoning skills, as you develop a sense of justice and start to understand morals.

Your emotions can become stronger too. Sometimes, you'll feel like everyone likes you, but other times, you may feel misunderstood or rejected. Regardless of how you feel, it's important you learn how to communicate this, and developing your social skills ensures you can do this effectively.

Social skills help improve your ability to learn and think, which means you can become more independent throughout your life. It also helps you to see others' points of view, increase your attention span, and face challenges in your education. Personally, it can also help you become more aware of who you are, which can help you feel a sense of belonging and acceptance.

Many young people who improve such skills at a younger age behave better and find they have sharper minds and senses, are more confident, and are able to verbalize and express themselves easily, which helps them deal with the situations they're faced with.

Activity #1 – Discovering Your Social Skills

Now, there are 16 key social skills discussed in this book, but you may not need to refine them all because you may have some good skills already. That's why your first activity before you continue reading this book is to learn how to assess your own social skills. All you need to do is complete the activity below, with your own social skills in mind:

List three things you do well... (What are you good at?)	*Why do you think you're good at the things you do well?*
1.	1.
2.	2.
3.	3.
(Example: *I am good at listening to others*)	(Example: *I don't interrupt when people are talking, and I listen carefully, interacting appropriately*)
List three things you need to improve... (What do you need to get better at?) 1. 2. 3. (Example: *I need to get better at making friends*)	*How can you work on the things you need to improve?* 1. 2. 3. (Example: *Practice what I will say when I meet new people, try the sports group I've been wanting to attend but have felt too shy to go, attempt to make new friends*)

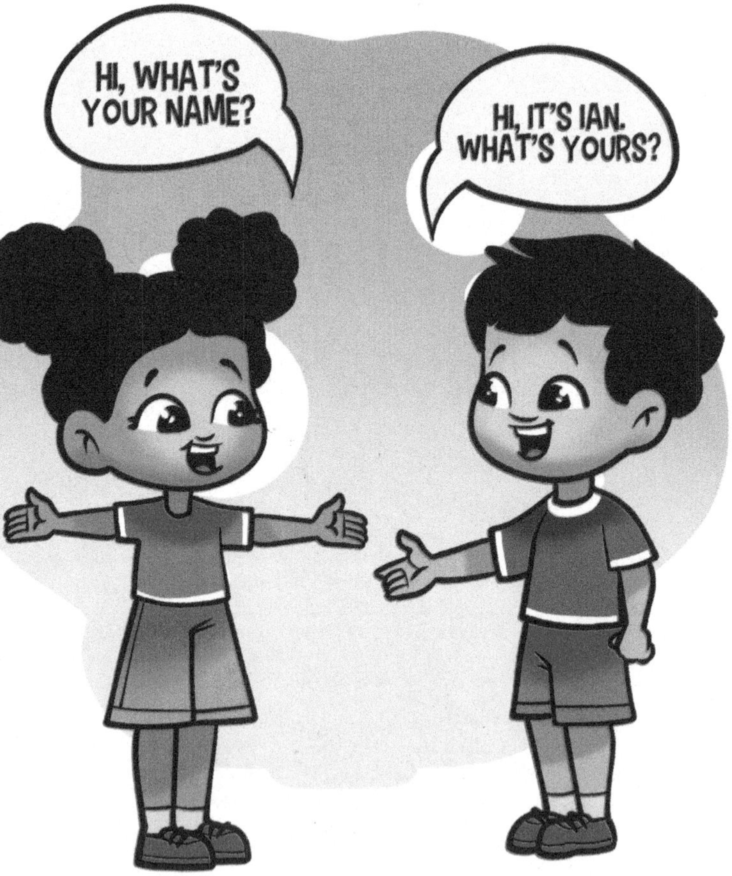
HI, WHAT'S YOUR NAME?
HI, IT'S IAN. WHAT'S YOURS?

Chapter 2:

When You Talk, What Do They Hear?

Do you ever get the feeling other people don't really listen when you talk?

Or maybe we should flip this...

When other people talk, do you really LISTEN?

It's common to feel like people, especially adults, don't really listen to you, but this is something that has to work both ways. This is communication!

You have to communicate effectively with others, and others have to communicate effectively with you too.

When we communicate, there are three different ways to do this. This can either be through verbal communication (speaking), through written communication (text or writing/typing), or non-verbal communication (which is neither written nor spoken – we'll explain this later in the chapter). Good communication is a two-way street, so listening is a critical component.

Communication is extremely important. That's why we'll focus on how you can communicate well while improving your listening skills, and all the appropriate non-verbal cues you can use and read when trying to get your message across to others. We'll then focus on some key tips to help you improve your general communication skills, so you can really get others to listen to what you have to say!

Let's find out why communication is so important...

Why Is Communication So Important?

Communication is the way you express a message to others. Having good communication will help you grow in confidence, and it can also help you develop relationships and set boundaries.

If you don't communicate well with others, how do you expect them to know what you're thinking?

Having good communication skills can help to:

★ Spark your imagination

★ Increase your ability to problem solve

★ Help you develop your independent thinking skills

★ Improve your literacy skills, language, and vocabulary

★ Develop and increase your self-esteem

★ Strengthen relationships with others

★ Learn order and discipline

★ Express yourself clearly

★ Improve your other social skills

Communication is a skill that everyone needs to develop and constantly improve, even adults, so reading this chapter will give you the head start you need.

When You Talk, What Do Others Hear?

Talking/speaking is verbal communication, so if you don't communicate what you want to say clearly, people could misunderstand you.

For example, if you don't explain to your mom that you no longer like chicken nuggets, *how will she know?* Saying something like, "I didn't feel like eating the chicken nuggets," or, "I didn't want them today," isn't exactly telling her that you've stopped liking them entirely and would prefer not to have them for dinner again. Your mom isn't psychic! You need to tell her in a clear way...

"Actually, mom, I haven't been enjoying chicken nuggets lately, so is it possible to have something else for dinner next time, please?"

Now, one thing I would remind you of when being direct is to remember your manners. We can express a message that we don't like something, while still being polite. Communication is even better if you're polite.

There are many things you can do to ensure you communicate well. For example, you should:

★ Open the conversation confidently

★ Speak slowly and clearly

★ Use appropriate language

★ Use your body language to strengthen your verbal message

★ Allow others to engage and ask questions, and listen to what they have to say

★ Take turns speaking if you are having a conversation.

If you feel like the people you're talking to aren't listening, it's okay for you to check that they are, in a respectful way. You could say, "Please, can you listen?", "It's really important that you listen," or, "Please listen carefully." You could also ask questions to ensure they understood what you said; for example, "Did you hear what time I said I have to be at band practice tomorrow?"

Now that you've mastered verbal communication, it's time to move on to non-verbal.

What Do You Say, When You Don't Say Anything?

Non-verbal communication is basically when you use things like gestures or the way you hold your body to communicate. This is also known as your body language or body cues. A fun fact is that 93% of all communication is non-verbal! With this in mind, our non-verbal communication can really strengthen our verbal communication.

Has your parent, teacher, or another adult ever looked at you, and you can tell they're proud of you, just from the way they look? Or maybe they've put their hands on their hips and made a facial expression that lets you know you're in trouble, even though they haven't said a word yet?

That's the power of non-verbal cues and communication!

Non-verbal communication includes the messages you send when you shrug, roll your eyes, smile, sigh, slouch, fold your arms, nod or shake your head, maintain or avoid eye contact. That's because the way you move your body, your gestures, and your facial expressions all give clues and strengthen what you're trying to say.

Touch is also an example of non-verbal communication. For example, we may place our hand on a person's arm to comfort them if they're upset, we shake hands with a person to welcome them, or we could pat them on the back to say, "good job."

Acknowledging space is another good non-verbal method of communication, as we should only use touch with people we are comfortable with. We don't want to intimidate another person by invading their space. Sometimes, invading a person's space is an act of bullying, and it's not okay to do that to others, or them to you. It's still important that you are able to read the signs, though, so if a person is trying to bully you, you can respond appropriately.

The way in which you say something, such as tone of voice, is also an example of non-verbal communication. Think about how you use your voice when you're happy, excited, sad, angry, or if you're being sarcastic. Your tone of voice can help you sound confident, too!

Now that we know all about non-verbal communication, let's look at written communication.

Written Communication

Written communication is when you write or type something onto a piece of paper or an electronic device. This can include:

★ A text message on your cellphone or using another messaging system, including social media or apps, through which you're communicating with another person

★ If you write a letter or create a poster that others will read

★ If you write a note to your mom to say you've gone to soccer practice

★ If you take a message from a person who called for your brother and leave it in a place where he can see it

Writing is a useful skill to have when communicating with others, but you need to do this clearly. When you are doing your schoolwork, or taking an exam or test, being able to write clearly can help you do well.

At your age, to develop your writing, you should:

★ Practice putting your ideas on paper. You could start by doing mind maps before you turn them into longer pieces of writing.

★ Read more. Reading helps to build your vocabulary and language skills.

★ Make a list of sentence starters that can help you if you later struggle to write. You can ask a parent, teacher, or another adult to help you.

A good way to check your writing is to read it out loud, so you can hear how your writing sounds to others. Even better, get a friend or an adult to read through it and give you some feedback to help you improve it.

When Others Talk, What Do You Hear?

A big part of being able to communicate well is to listen. If you want to become a good communicator, you must make sure you are a good listener.

Being a good listener means:

★ Not interrupting a person while they are talking

★ Maintaining eye contact

★ Repeating back what the person has said (when it's appropriate)

★ Asking questions if you're unclear

Active listening can help you become better at solving problems, and it can ensure there are fewer misunderstandings when you communicate with others. If you don't listen well, it's really difficult for you to know what others expect from you.

Everyone develops at their own rate, but at your age, it's expected that you can understand what others are trying to say and have the confidence to ask questions if you don't understand.

How to Improve Communication Skills

Boosting your communication skills can help you develop confidence in every future interaction. Practice and experience will make you a better communicator overall.

1. Practice speaking in environments you're comfortable with and, once you do this well, start to challenge yourself to speak in group settings. For example, you can describe your day to people in your family.

2. Practice your listening skills by asking your family members about their day and asking questions when necessary.

3. Make an effort to talk to others, such as your neighbors or friends, even if you're just asking how they are.

4. Listen and reflect on what you've said. Ask yourself:
   a. Could you have said anything differently?
   b. How could you improve that communication?

5. Don't be afraid to take time to think about your answers when you've been asked a question. We all need some thinking time, and this will help to develop your thinking skills, and reply more appropriately.

6. Reflect on your writing by going back to something you wrote last week, and then this week, and spend time improving it. You can do this by:
   a. Checking your spelling
   b. Checking your punctuation
   c. Swapping some of the words you've used for other words

7. Read a book. Remember, reading improves your vocabulary and language skills. Practice reading quietly and reading aloud.

Activity #2 – Describing Activity

The describing activity is a great way to help you improve your communication skills. You should:

1. Choose an object (any object – this can be something you have in your bedroom, such as a toy)

2. Describe it in writing – write down a description of the item using your senses; what does it look like, feel like, smell like, does it make a sound?

3. Now, describe it to another person (by talking)

4. Ask the other person to describe it (is there anything they said that you hadn't?)

5. Go back to your written description and improve it. What could you say differently? How could you improve your writing?

Chapter 3:

Let's Talk About How You Feel

How would you like to be happy more often?

Emotions are difficult. Sometimes, you are happy, but other times, you are sad. Then sometimes, you have feelings you don't really understand.

Don't worry; this is normal! It is part of growing up, and as you start to know more about yourself, you can start to tap into the emotions that make you feel good more often.

Do you ever feel like crying but don't know why? Or feel extremely angry or happy, yet you don't know what's causing this? You can learn to figure this out by becoming more emotionally aware. This will help you to learn how to manage your emotions, regulate them, and feel more in control. It can help you develop your overall emotional intelligence.

It's common to experience emotional and social changes, and right now, you're probably aware of peer pressure. Your friendships may become more complex, you have deep bonds with your close friends, and it's likely you pay more attention to what you look like and notice how your body is changing as you grow. With that in mind, this chapter will look at how you can assess how you feel, the benefits of managing your emotions, as well as looking at how you can regulate your emotions. We'll also explore how you can be patient and gain more self-control.

Let's get started!

How Do You Feel?

When people talk about emotions, they're talking about how you feel inside, and the way you feel about things that happen to you. There are six basic emotions that we'll concentrate on in this chapter, which are:

1. Happiness
2. Sadness
3. Anger
4. Fear
5. Surprise
6. Disgust

They are your primary emotions, but of course, there are more complex emotions attached to these, so let's look at each.

If a person is happy, they could feel joyful, optimistic, or proud. A person who is sad may have feelings of guilt or boredom, or they could even be lonely.

When a person is angry, they could feel hurt, mad, depressed, or even threatened, and when they're fearful, it's possible that they feel anxious, insecure, or even scared.

A person who is surprised could be excited, amazed, or maybe even startled, while a person who feels disgusted is often disappointed, and may even have feelings that cause them to disapprove of or avoid a certain person, thing, or situation.

I'm sure you can think of many more emotions you've experienced, which is great, because the more aware you are of your emotions, the more emotionally competent you become. Being emotionally competent means you can deal with the emotions you experience well, because you understand them, and therefore, you can express

your feelings appropriately. This doesn't have to be complicated, and you're doing this already if you:

★ Smile when you're happy

★ Cry when you're upset

★ Fold your arms when you're unhappy

★ Jump up and down or giggle when you're excited

Because all these things (and many more, as I'm sure you have your own examples) are natural non-verbal responses that show the emotions you're experiencing.

Now, the more aware you are, the more you can monitor your own emotions, as well as the emotions of other people. You can then learn how to use your emotions to guide how you think or act. A child with higher emotional intelligence is able to pay better attention, is more engaged in school, is often more empathetic, and is more likely to have a positive relationship with others.

Let's talk more about emotional intelligence!

Emotional Intelligence

Emotional intelligence is when you respect others' feelings, can manage and express your own feelings, and use them to guide what you do next or in the future. For instance, if a person makes you angry, and you can calm yourself down, that's a great skill. This is because you're in tune with your emotions and recognize that getting angry will not solve the problem. It's still important that you can express yourself in a healthy way, maybe by talking calmly or assertively about the issue, rather than screaming and shouting. It also shapes how you think.

There are many benefits to developing your emotional intelligence; for example, it can improve your mental health and well-being, help you develop deeper relationships with your friends and family, help you perform better so you get higher grades, and therefore have more chances of success in the future.

The good news is that you can develop this by learning how to manage your emotions.

The Benefits of Managing Your Emotions

You're probably wondering why there's so much hype around managing your emotions, and before you continue, it's important to clarify the benefits. That's because if you do, you are more likely to:

★ Feel more secure
★ Increase your self-confidence
★ Act in calm and healthy ways
★ Become better at problem-solving
★ Feel loved and know your worth
★ Learn from your mistakes

Now that you know the benefits, let's explore how you can begin to regulate your emotions.

Regulating Your Emotions

At your age, you should be able to recognize how certain emotions impact your behavior. Therefore, you can practice regulating them. To do this, you should first calm your mind by either:

★ Practicing deep breathing – inhale through your nose for the count of four and then breathe out fully until all the air has left your lungs. This can be useful if you feel anxious, stressed, or angry.

★ Allowing yourself some time to take a break from what you're doing. Go for a walk, get a drink of water, or take yourself off to your room for some alone time to think.

★ Distracting yourself by counting down from 10 to 1, or a higher number if necessary.

The best thing to do to get to the bottom of your emotions is to journal. This is a book you dedicate to writing down your feelings, thoughts, and behaviors so you can examine them.

Once you've calmed down, it's time to identify the emotion. *How do you feel?* Start with the six basic emotions and go from there. Write it all in your journal.

Let's say you are angry because your sister went into your room and borrowed something without asking.

Once you've identified your emotion, you need to problem-solve the issue by considering what triggered that emotion. *What was happening just before you experienced that emotion?*

So, if we go back to the example, you get home and notice your item is missing. You then find it in your sister's room.

Now it's time to think about what it was that made you so angry.

On this occasion, you're angry because your sister went into your room and took your item without asking. This isn't the first time, and you've asked her not to, but she keeps doing it. You feel like she doesn't respect your privacy or your things.

Then, you need to consider what you can do to control that emotion or make it better, rather than dwelling on it. You need to think about:

- ★ How bad is it, really, now that you've calmed your mind?
- ★ What made you feel this emotion so strongly?
- ★ What would have been a better scenario?
- ★ Can you come to any compromise?
- ★ How can you express how you feel (to your sister, in our example)?
- ★ What would make you feel better right now?

Once you start to be more aware of your emotions, you can recognize them, assess them, and really put them into perspective. It isn't always easy to keep your emotions under control, but this is something you can learn to do, and it helps you to be more self-aware.

You could also create a calm-down kit, filled with some things that cheer you up. This could be coloring books, a journal, a soft toy, a stress ball, scratch-and-sniff stickers, or a lavender pillow. Engaging your senses can help you manage your emotions, so don't forget to journal everything too.

Learning patience is a great way to develop your emotional intelligence, too!

Being Patient

You probably feel like you want to do the things you want to do right away. You want to buy the latest tech right now, you want the new outfit or shoes now, and you want to visit your favorite theme park or go on holiday now. But patience is important.

I bet your parents or other adults in your life have told you to "be patient."

That's because there are so many benefits to being patient. These include learning to take turns, being grateful, strengthening relationships, and providing you with a learning opportunity, so you can improve your social skills and behavior.

If you want to learn patience, you should observe how other family members respond in situations that require it. For example, your parents have to wait in line at the grocery store every time they go to buy food. Observe how they handle that and learn from them.

Practice waiting. Learning to wait isn't always easy, but it's something that will help you in the long term. *Have you ever heard the expression, "good things come to those who wait?"* That's because waiting is an art. It takes time to get used to waiting. Think of waiting for cookies to bake in the oven – the excitement of making them, the smell, then, finally, the taste. The anticipation of waiting for something good makes us grateful and excited!

It's a good idea to set a timescale when you're teaching yourself patience, and also visualize what happens if you don't wait. If someone didn't wait in line at the store and pushed in front of you, *how would you feel?* If you took the cookies out of the oven too early, they wouldn't be edible. Visualize it, then think about *how you would feel.*

The truth is, you're getting older now, and you have to learn patience. So keep practicing, as this can help with self-control.

Self-Control Tips

Now, it's not always easy to have full self-control, but there are some ways to gain control of your emotions, so let's explore how you can alter your emotions:

- ★ If you wake up in the morning and you're feeling tired and moody, you could do some exercise
- ★ If you start to feel sad, you could do something that makes you happy
- ★ If you have some homework to do, but you're not motivated, reward yourself when you've done it, and reward consistency
- ★ If you're feeling upset, talk to a friend or family member and ask them to listen or help you figure it out

Self-control can help you improve your willpower and self-discipline, and it can also help you focus.

Activity #3 – Assessing Your Emotions

It's important that you check in with yourself and assess your emotions. Follow the exercise below. All you need is a piece of paper and a pencil, and if you have a journal, you can use that:

1. Close your eyes and take three deep breaths, breathing in through your nose for a count of four, and out through your mouth until you've blown out all the air you can.
2. Draw a circle on your piece of paper.
3. *How do you feel?* Draw the facial expression of how you feel within your circle.
4. Either above or below the circle, write down three things you can do that make you happy.
5. Choose one of those things to do today – choose happiness!

Now that you've learned how to better manage your emotions, you can start to use these skills. We've already mentioned how this can help strengthen relationships, so next, let's talk about making friends.

Chapter 4:

Making Friends

"There is nothing on this earth more to be prized than true friendship."
~ Thomas Aquinas

There's nothing more precious than friends, but making new friends and being a good friend to the friends you have isn't always easy. Occasionally, friendships can be challenging, as sometimes we grow apart from others or we don't always see eye-to-eye.

Like communication, friendship requires give and take. You need to be a good friend, but you also need to have good friends. But *what does it mean to be a "good friend?"*

In this chapter, we'll find out. We'll talk about making friends and keeping them, as well as looking at what it means to be a good friend and the importance of friendships. We'll also have the opportunity to discuss managing conflict!

How to Make Friends and Keep Them

For some, making friends is something they can do without thinking about it, but for others, it's more complex. If you have to make new friends now, it could possibly take you out of your comfort zone, but if you're prepared, it can boost your confidence in such situations.

Watch your friends and family and notice how they interact with others. With friends, neighbors, yourself, and even the staff in the local grocery store.

Think about how you can approach others when you visit somewhere new...

What would you say?

You could start by making a list of all the things you like. It could be sports, hobbies, school subjects, books, TV shows, movies, celebrities, crafts, and even food or your favorite restaurants. Your list gives you some ideas of topics you can talk about.

Even if you find social situations difficult, it's important that you don't avoid them. Set yourself some achievable goals, so you have something to aim for. Try asking a friend or a family member to help, and practice role-play scenarios with them. Just choose a topic to talk about!

As a rule of thumb, it's a good idea to introduce yourself when you first meet someone, so think of something interesting to say to them. Now, it's okay if you don't hit it off with everyone. While we should be kind to everyone, not everyone becomes our friend. It's common for us to make friends with people if we have similar interests.

All that's left to do is to become good friends over time by getting to know each other. But *what exactly is a good friend?*

How to Be a Good Friend

There are no set rules for what makes a good friend, as we all have our own individual expectations of what we expect of a friend. *Think... What's important to you when it comes to your friends?*

In order to be a good friend, you should:

★ Make your friends happy, by making them feel good about themselves. Give them compliments and congratulate them on their achievements.

★ Support them. Just be there for them when they need it, especially if they're feeling low.

★ Listen to your friends. Don't interrupt them and give them your full attention.

★ Show them they can trust you. This means, if they tell you a secret, don't tell anyone, and don't judge them.

★ Encourage your friends. Remember, while you will have some things in common, you don't have to have everything in common. So, if they have a different interest to you, encourage them. Don't be afraid to do your own thing too.

★ Handle any conflict respectfully. You don't always have to agree on everything, but if you do say something out of order, don't be afraid to apologize. Also, if your friend upsets you, be honest and tell them. A good friend will listen to your concerns.

★ Remember that good friendship is a two-way street, so make sure the person to whom you are a good friend is also a good friend to you.

★ Have more than one friend. While it's okay to have a best friend, there's no reason you can't have a group of friends. In fact, it's a great idea. Having more than one friend ensures you're not limiting your options.

★ You don't need followers. Social media means we can feel pressured to have a lot of friends. These people may not be real friends, but simply followers, so make sure you know the difference between the two and keep your information and thoughts private (solely for true friends who care about you). *But how do you know who really cares?*

How to Choose Your Friends

Choosing the right friends isn't easy, especially when you're young. That's because many of us start out thinking we're friends with everyone. That's a nice notion, and there are people who are easy to get along with and have lots of friends, but many people simply have a small circle of close friends. But *how do you choose who should be in your close circle of friends?*

1. Choose friends who have similar interests or beliefs as you – people you have something in common with.

2. Choose friends who make you feel good – the last thing you need is a friend who puts you down.

3. Choose friends who make time for you and give good advice when you need it – we need people to talk to, so a good friend will make time for you, and you should make time for them too.

4. Choose friends who encourage and motivate you – your friends should be your biggest cheerleaders.

5. Choose friends who bring out the best in you, not the worst. Hang out with people who are well-behaved, good for you, and who want you to do the right things.

6. Choose friends who want you to succeed. Good friends want you to do well in life, so when you do something amazing or achieve something, they'll be happy for you – not jealous!

7. Choose friends who understand you – having a friend that gets you is important. We all have different personalities, and our friends should understand who we are and connect with us.

8. Choose friends who want you as a friend, too –make sure when you're a friend to a person, they are a friend to you too.

Now choosing a friend is great, but *what happens if your friend stops being a good friend?*

What if I Have a Bad Friend?

If a friendship is not making you happy, you may need to take a step back. While we can have jokes with our friends, sometimes it goes too far. There's a difference between having fun and making fun of someone.

Someone is not being a good friend to you if you find they are:

★ Saying unkind or hurtful things to you, but claiming they're only being honest

★ Putting you down

★ Telling other people things about you when you've asked them not to

★ Pressuring you to do things you don't want to do

★ Trying to manipulate you

★ Talking about you in a negative way to others

★ Excluding you from group activities on purpose

★ Laughing at you and trying to get others to laugh at you too

This is actually bullying behavior. If your friend is doing this, you should talk to them about how you feel, but remember; you are not the problem.

When you approach your friend and tell them how you feel, the way they respond will give you a clue as to whether they're a good friend or not. If they say sorry and stop doing these things, then they are a good friend. If they try to blame you for their behavior, tell you it's fun, or suggest that you are wrong to overreact, it could be time to take a step back from the friendship.

Many people worry about confronting their friends when they feel upset because they're worried about causing conflict. Let's talk about that!

Managing Conflict

Sometimes, you will encounter conflict with friends – this is normal. To keep things calm and avoid further conflict, you should avoid name-calling and hurtful words. When expressing how you feel, use "I" statements to explain.

Conflict happens because there's a problem, so you need to try and solve it. But first, you need to figure out what originally caused the problem. To do this, you need to talk to the person you have the conflict with.

Try to figure out a solution that would be best for you both, and be willing to compromise. This means, sometimes you don't get exactly what you want, but neither does the other person – you meet in the middle.

When the other person is talking, make sure you listen carefully and look them in the eye. Remember, active listening means you don't interrupt. Regardless of what the other person says, you should keep being kind. This can be difficult, but don't let conflict with another person change who you are.

Try your best to be flexible and reach an agreement. It's best to resolve the problem, rather than letting the conflict continue, but handling conflict can be stressful. If you feel you need some help or advice, speak to an adult, a family member, or a friend you can trust.

Others can be positive role models for you, and they can create a safe environment that helps you express yourself. They can help you figure out what you want and talk through how you can handle the situation.

Managing conflict and friendships is something everyone experiences, and everyone's experience is different. I believe in you – there's nothing you can't figure out!

Activity #4 – What Makes a Good Friend?

Only you can decide what you need in a friend, so start to think about this.

★ Brain-dump the things you think you need from a friend. *Do you want kindness, to be supported, someone who listens to you, etc?*

★ Make a list of your good qualities – *how are you a good friend?*

If you want your new friend to become a close friend, this can take some time. Making friends involves using the skills you've already learned in this book prior to this chapter, such as communicating well and managing your emotions, but most of all, it requires patience. Remember, everyone deserves good friends, so don't be or accept anything less.

Chapter 5:

Getting Along With Others

As you go through a typical day, think about all the people you encounter...

This is a long list for most of us, starting with parents, brothers or sisters, neighbors, teachers, and friends, as well as other people you come across throughout your day.

Now, do you get along with everyone you encounter?

You see, there are people we meet with whom we don't have things in common, which means we can find it difficult to get along with them. But sometimes, we need to get along with people for many different reasons. *How do you cooperate with them, or help them?*

As we journey through our life, we have to learn to get along with others. It's all part of being a good citizen, and these skills can be taken with you throughout your life, as you head into your teens, and then your adult life.

This chapter will focus on the different ways you can help others, how to increase your cooperation skills, and how you can collaborate better with others. We'll also talk about people we may not get along with.

Mastering each of these will help you get along with others, and there are many benefits of doing so. Let's explore some of these benefits.

The Benefits of Getting Along With Others

It's really important that you learn to get along with others because:

★ It improves your overall social skills, so social environments can become easier for you.

- ★ It helps to strengthen your other social skills and abilities, such as empathy, knowing right from wrong, and the ability to understand the perspective of another person.
- ★ It helps you develop how to communicate in a polite way.
- ★ It ensures you develop your listening skills.
- ★ It encourages you to cooperate better with others.
- ★ It helps to strengthen your self-control and your ability to resolve conflict.
- ★ If you feel uncomfortable or unsure in certain social situations, getting along with others eases that feeling, and enables you to communicate how you feel.

If you master getting along with others, you will develop all the social skills above too, and this will make social situations so much easier for you in the future.

What Happens if I Don't Get Along With Someone?

You're probably wondering what happens when you don't get along with others. The truth is that you would have difficulty making friends, strengthening relationships, and communicating effectively, and this could impact your overall social life.

If you don't get along with people and you allow this to impact your behavior, it could affect your relationships and education. You don't need to be friends with everyone, but you should be able to get along with anyone. That doesn't mean you have to agree with or believe in everything that they do, but you should be respectful and polite.

If you don't get along with someone, ask yourself why not and think about the ways you can still communicate as you need to. You should keep your interactions brief if necessary, and you should consider their perspective too. *How do you think that person feels in their situation?*

If you don't try to get along with others, others may find it difficult to get along with you, and this can impact several aspects of your life, including your social life, family, and educational time. Getting along with as many people as possible brings peace and harmony into your life and prevents your judgment from being clouded.

Let's talk about how you can get along with others by helping and cooperating, as these are key skills you require.

Tips for Helping Others

Helping others shows the type of person you are. Being helpful is a great skill a person can acquire. It means being useful to, or providing assistance to others, which can make you feel happier, and empowers you to take on more responsibilities.

There are lots of ways to help others, support your community, and generally be a good citizen. For instance, maybe you can:

★ Help your friend with their homework
★ Help your mom with the dishes
★ Take the trash out for your dad
★ Help your elderly neighbor do some gardening
★ Pick up litter in your neighborhood or community

There are five things you can do if you want to help others. These are:

1. Being more mindful of others and considering what you can do that will make things easier for another person.

2. Making a list of the people in your life, and then brainstorming the different ways you can help them.

3. Setting a goal to help at least one person each day.

4. Talking through your ideas for helping with family and friends.

5. Asking others how they would like you to help them.

Once you're thinking more about helping others, you should also consider the different ways you cooperate with others. *Let's talk about that further...*

Cooperation Skills

When we talk about cooperating, do you know what that really means?

Cooperation means working with others to achieve a common goal. So, let's say you have a school project that a group of you need to complete. Each member of the group has a job to do. If everyone does their job and cooperates, you will get a good grade! This benefits you, the other members of your group, and your teacher.

When you are young, you learn to share and play with other children, and this is the beginning of your ability to cooperate. It grows from there. There are some things you can do to practice your cooperation skills, too. For example, you could:

★ Play a game that involves taking turns talking (like performing a play, role playing, singing a song in which everyone sings a verse, or presenting information to your class).

★ Donate something you believe someone else would like. For example, if you grow out of a toy you loved as a child, you could donate it to another young child who you believe would enjoy it.

★ Compete in a relay race and cheer on your team.

Cooperation is a key soft skill for you to develop, and it's part of the bigger picture when it comes to helping you get along with others.

Now it's time to practice and grow those skills, so you can continue to work with others.

Activity #5 – Thinking It Out

Have a look at some of the scenarios below and consider what you've learned about getting along with others.

Scenario #1 – Helping Others

Your neighbor is unwell. They are elderly and live on their own. The trash will be collected in your neighborhood today.

What three things could you do to help them?

Scenario #2 –Cooperating With Others

The local school is having a fundraising event to raise money for a local children's charity. Your sister said you need to donate something, and you agree to cooperate.

What would you donate and why?

Scenario #3 – Good Sportsmanship

You compete in a sports day. There are 20 people in your race. You win the 100-meter sprint, and your friend comes second. Your other friend comes sixth.

How would you show 'good sportsmanship'?

There's no doubt that helping others and cooperating ensures you get along well with the people in your life. If you can do that while also communicating effectively, making friends, and being able to manage your emotions, you're well on your way to mastering your social skills. We've already talked briefly about problem-solving, but because it's so important, we've dedicated Chapter 6 to it.

Let's talk about solving problems!

Chapter 6:

How to Solve a Problem

"The problem is not the problem. The problem is your attitude about the problem." ~Captain Jack Sparrow

Sometimes, we have a problem we need to overcome. Oftentimes, we need several skills to do this, because problem-solving doesn't simply involve a single skill, but many. This includes learning to assess the situation in order to figure out what to do.

How would you like to learn the skills that allow you to do this?

When we learn to overcome problems, we can tweak our negotiating skills, and we can also make informed decisions. But solving a problem can be a challenge. Therefore, being able to solve a problem involves requires you to have the right attitude, just like Captain Jack Sparrow suggests above.

Attitude is a major part of problem-solving, because you need to be in the right mindset; otherwise, your efforts to resolve issues are at risk of failure.

In this chapter, we'll shift the attention to problem-solving, overcoming barriers, and building negotiating skills. We'll also talk about how this leads to good decision-making, which is covered in more detail in Chapter 7. It's important that you know and understand what a problem is, and when to take action. Let's clarify this first!

When Is a Problem a Problem?

We are all faced with problems in our lives. A problem is a situation or matter that you need to deal with, because it's not the outcome you desire and may be harmful. Sometimes, a problem causes stress, doubt, or difficulty, which means we must find a solution. We often need to find a way around or a way to overcome the problem or settle on a compromise, and this is how we resolve it.

It's likely that, at your age, you've encountered a problem that has upset you, angered you, or caused you stress. If something didn't disrupt a situation or how you felt, it wouldn't be a problem. Unfortunately, they are a part of life that we must learn to deal with, and some problems or solutions become lessons — they teach us valuable lessons and strengthen some of our soft skills.

If you can solve problems on your own, this shows how independent you are becoming. The younger you are when you develop your problem-solving skills, the better, as doing this also means you're less likely to feel frustrated or disheartened when faced with problems.

When you get older, you'll find that you problem-solve daily in your education, work life, or at home, which is why this is such an important life skill. Problems should be looked at positively, because if you can resolve them effectively and efficiently, it can help increase your resilience, and improve your perseverance. It also builds character because it provides you with the opportunity to expand your thinking skills.

Let's take a moment to discuss problem-solving and the role your attitude plays in this.

Attitude and Problem-Solving

We mentioned in the introduction that attitude is vital when it comes to problem-solving, so let's take a moment to consider this. If you try to solve problems but start off believing you won't succeed, then it can be difficult to put the required effort into resolving the issues.

Having a positive approach to problem-solving improves your confidence, your willingness, and your perseverance. That's because your attitude will empower you to succeed and help you solve problems as quickly as possible.

A problem is best approached with a clear mind. When you're solving a problem, you also need to remain open-minded, because lacking flexibility can lead to coming up with the wrong solution.

If you don't have the right attitude and don't believe you will find a solution, it can lead to lower productivity and morale. Having a bad day can cloud your judgment and make it impossible for you to solve a problem effectively.

If you want success when it comes to solving problems and overcoming obstacles, you must maintain a positive attitude – it helps you get the success you want and deserve.

Did you know a positive attitude is sometimes called a "can-do" attitude?

But how can you maintain a positive, can-do attitude? You can:

1. Celebrating your wins and positive experiences.
2. Helping others – try to help at least one person, once per day, as this impacts how you feel.

3. Reflecting on all the good things that have happened and all the things you're grateful for.

4. Trying meditations that focus on love and kindness.

5. Being encouraged by others, such as your friends, family, a coach, or your teachers.

6. Taking on new responsibilities and achieving them.

7. Setting goals that are realistic and achievable, so you know you can accomplish them.

Staying positive can be a challenge, but it really helps you keep the frame of mind you need to solve problems effectively (and much more).

"Try to be a rainbow in someone's cloud." ~ Maya Angelou

Overcoming Barriers

Imagine you're walking down a quiet road and then you must stop because a tree has fallen over. It's blocking your path. *What would you do?*

You see the tree is a barrier. It's stopping you from carrying out your journey in the way you first planned. A barrier is really a simple problem, but it's something you need to figure out, and in most cases, you can do that quickly.

When we are faced with such a barrier, we automatically try to think of how we can carry on with what we planned to do with minimal disruption. Those automatic thoughts and actions are our own personal approach.

Now let's think of different ways you can overcome barriers...

1. **Assessing the Situation** – You first have to assess the situation and how complex it is. Let's consider the fallen tree again.

You would think about the danger it poses and the easiest way to overcome it, in order to be able to get on with your journey again as quickly as possible.

2. **Setting Goals** – If you need to overcome a barrier and it's quite complex, then you may need to set goals to help you. Think about the ideal outcome – that's your goal. You then need to set smaller steps to help you achieve your goal. In the case of the fallen tree, let's say it's in a dangerous position and it needs to be moved, as it could cause an accident. While your goal is to get back on your journey, you also know you need to do the right thing and keep others safe. With that in mind, there are things you must do in order to achieve your goal, so your smaller steps could be to:

   a. Report the fallen tree to the authorities
   b. Warn passersby of the dangers of the tree while you wait for the authorities to make sure everyone stays safe
   c. When the relevant authorities arrive to move the tree and take over the scene, get back to your journey

3. **Asking for Advice or Help** – Good news! You don't have to face every barrier you encounter alone. It's okay to ask others for advice; in fact, asking others for help makes you stronger. You could ask your friends, your family, your teacher, or another adult you know who is suited to solving your problem. This is beneficial because it helps you learn how others would resolve problems, which then teaches you different perspectives and solutions. You can also observe how other people in your life overcome the barriers they face. *How would your friend, family member, teacher, or neighbor get past the fallen tree?*

4. **Use Your Strengths** – When overcoming a barrier, it's good to use your strengths. Let's consider the fallen tree again. If you're good at climbing, you could climb over it. If you're good at fitting through small spaces and crawling, you could go under it. If you're not good at any of those things, but staying safe is a priority, you could go around it, because even though it will take a little longer, it's safer, and your logic is your strength.

Problem-Solving 101

Now, some problems aren't as simple as physical barriers blocking your path. They take much more investigation and require more thought and clarity. Learning to solve problems takes practice, but in order to practice, you need to know what to do. Earlier in this chapter, we talked about our automatic response to problem-solving or overcoming barriers, which is ultimately our own personal problem-solving process. Let's look at some techniques to help you understand the process of solving a problem.

There are five key steps to problem-solving:

1. **Describe the Problem Exactly** – You must have a clear understanding of what the problem is. Let's say you want to bake a cake, but you are missing one of the ingredients. Describing the problem would indicate exactly what the problem is and provide specific details. For example, the problem could be that you can't make a cake because you don't have any eggs. It's that simple – describe the problem but don't make it complicated.

2. **Gather Information About the Problem** – Who does it affect and how? So, not having eggs affects you because you can't make the cake. It also affects anyone with whom you are going to share the cake with.

3. **Make a List of Possible Solutions** – Sometimes, the problem takes more thought because there are other things to consider. For instance, you may think about buying or borrowing some eggs. Or, you could change your recipe and make a cake that doesn't require eggs.

4. **Assess or Evaluate Your Possible Solutions** – For example, the easiest solution to the missing eggs would be to buy more. However, if the store is far away, you're not allowed to go alone, or you don't have any money for eggs, it may not be possible. Another solution would be to borrow them from your neighbor. If you need them quickly, the neighbor may be the best option for you.

5. **Choose Your Solution and Check That It Worked** – For example, if you choose to borrow from your neighbor, you can bake the cake. If the neighbor doesn't have (enough) eggs, you then need to reassess your other options and choose another solution.

Problem-solving isn't always straightforward, and sometimes you'll try something, and it won't work, but this adds to your learning. You just have to reflect on why it didn't work and re-evaluate a solution that might work. This is a learning curve for you and will strengthen your ability to solve problems in the future. There are occasions when you have to involve other people in making your way to a solution too, and sometimes that involves a concept we've mentioned before... *Negotiation!*

Let's explore that further.

How to Negotiate Like a Pro

Being able to negotiate is another great social skill that will help you throughout the entirety of your life, and it's a key part of problem-solving. Sometimes, you need to have the confidence to ask questions and debate, so you can gain a deeper understanding and persuade or argue your point of view.

If you're wondering what it means to negotiate, it's basically a discussion between at least two people that helps them come to an agreement. Many people imagine negotiations as being an argument, but the key to good negotiation is to stay calm.

By the time you're a teenager, negotiation skills are common, and you will have had time to practice your ability to negotiate. Some great ways to do this are to:

★ Ask your parents, teachers, other family members, or friends how they arrived at an everyday decision. If they can explain it to you, you can start to understand their decision-making process.

★ Imagine having to negotiate a raise in your allowance. *What would you say? How could you make valid points?*

★ Don't be emotionally attached to your points of view. Try arguing based on facts and evidence only, and try not to get emotional. If it makes you feel stressed, angry, or frustrated, you could talk to an adult about how you feel and why you feel that way.

★ Try to find common ground. If you start with something you can agree on, you can work from there.

★ When negotiating, make sure you listen actively to the other person. Everyone should have a chance to talk.

★ Sometimes, compromise is required on both sides. It's about give and take. Think about what you really need to achieve and see if there's a compromise that can be made.

Negotiation skills are excellent life skills that complement many other skills. We often find we can practice our negotiation when playing games, such as Monopoly. Empathy plays a big part in negotiating too, because you're a better negotiator when you can empathize with others, and it also increases your ability to understand others, which develops your emotional intelligence. This can help you to work through any disagreements or conflicts you face.

When you negotiate, it's important you recognize that negotiations don't necessarily result in a winner and loser. Sometimes they result in an outcome that benefits everyone. Every person's perspective should be considered before you reach a conclusion and, in order to do this, everyone should take an open-minded approach.

Being a good negotiator allows you to stand up for what you believe in and helps you develop the self-confidence you need to succeed. Being able to negotiate in a calm way that doesn't sacrifice your integrity or relationships will have a positive impact on your life and help you to earn respect from the people around you, but also ensure you respect others.

There's no doubt negotiation helps you grow personally, by helping you think in a more creative way that can aid decision-making in the future. We'll talk about that in more detail in the next chapter.

Let's apply your ability to problem-solve to real life.

1. Think of a problem you need to resolve or a problem you recently resolved.
2. Put the problem into words – explain it out loud.
3. Follow the five steps to problem-solving.

Problem-solving skills are really underrated, so please remember that they are super important. They help you:

★ Tap into your assessment and evaluation skills
★ Make good decisions
★ Cope with everyday challenges
★ Encounter difficulties with confidence
★ Increase your independence
★ Broaden your ability to think
★ Improve and strengthen other soft skills, such as your critical thinking and cooperation skills

Problem-solving is an essential skill that will develop throughout adulthood. There's no harm in getting started now, because the sooner you learn, the better you will get at it. Solving problems plays a big part in decision-making, so let's move on to that now.

Chapter 7:

Making Good Decisions

What does it mean to make a good decision?

You are faced with choices every day, which means you have decisions to make. You may choose what food you eat, what toy you play with, what game you play, what clothes you wear, whether to do your homework or not...

Your parents probably say you have to do the right thing, but *how do you know what that is? How do you know if you're making the right or wrong choice?* Especially if the choice you must make is a difficult one.

This chapter will focus on decision-making, and we'll talk about good versus bad decisions. We'll also talk about the importance of making good decisions, and how we can make them for ourselves.

Sometimes, we make mistakes and make bad decisions. It happens from time to time. With that in mind, this chapter also provides some important advice on what to do if you make a bad decision.

Let's go into more detail...

How Do We Know if It's a Good or Bad Decision?

A good decision is when you have options, but you make the best choice to achieve the best outcome. For example, you have homework due tomorrow, but you really want to go to the movies with your friend. You must decide what to do.

A good decision would be to do your homework and go to the movies another evening. Your homework is your responsibility, so even though you would like to see a movie, doing your homework is much more important. It means you won't get into trouble at school, you keep working on your education and grades, and you won't get into trouble with your parents.

A bad decision would be to go to the movies and not do your homework. This is because it means you're not prioritizing your education, which is important. You can visit the movie theater at any time, but you're on a deadline with your homework.

If we had a magic wand, we could wave it to ensure we always make the right decision. But making a decision is much more complicated, and sometimes it's impossible to know if you are making a good or bad decision.

★ Use your intuition – You've been guided by others in your life, so you already have a sense of what's right and wrong. This means you probably have a feeling or a little voice inside your head that guides you and reminds you what feels right. Sometimes we complicate a problem by overthinking how we should handle it. Although some problems require more consideration, some can be solved reasonably quickly.

★ "What if" – Think about the different decisions you could make and think about what could happen in each case. Just ask yourself, "What if I did this?"

★ Take yourself out of the equation – Sometimes, our decisions are personal, which makes it difficult for us to be logical. Take yourself out of the equation by imagining your friend has the same problem you do. *What would you tell them to do?*

Why Is It Important to Make Good Decisions?

As you get older, it becomes more and more important for you to master the skill of good decision-making. Although you have some things to learn, it's not as overwhelming as you may believe because your parents, teachers, and other adults in your life have been preparing you to make good decisions all your life. They've done this when they've:

★ Guided you to make the right choice

★ Asked your opinion, what you would do, or what you think

★ Taught you right from wrong

★ Talked to you about your behavior

★ Had conversations with you about a situation you could've handled differently

The older you get, the more complex problems you face, and therefore, the decisions you have to make become more difficult. This often means you have to compromise or negotiate with others. If you're good at making decisions, it means:

★ You can become more independent

★ You feel more confident

★ You are showing maturity, because you're willing to compromise

★ You are good at communicating your side, while listening to others

★ You can deal with poor decisions, make uncomfortable decisions, and learn from them

★ You have good thinking skills and you are encouraged to think ahead

★ You feel empowered, so you can go on to make more good choices in the future

★ You learn about the consequences of your actions

★ You can learn and grow as a person, the more you utilize your skills and learn from them

Making decisions is a learning curve, and while it means you can make your own choices, others can help you if a particular problem or issue is causing you stress or anxiety. You should never suffer in silence, because the adults in your life can guide you or support you in making the right choice. If you make the wrong decision, you can reflect on this, and think about what you would do differently in the future.

Making good decisions only leads to good things!

How to Make Good Decisions

Now, you're not going to master good decision-making overnight. It takes time; in fact, you should still be prepared for when you will make a bad decision from time to time as an adult. The more you experience decision-making, and you grow to learn to review things from different perspectives, the better you'll become.

When you're faced with an important decision, you'll need to answer some key questions:

1. Why do you want to do this? – It's essential that you begin to understand what motivates your decisions. It's likely you'll know why you made a particular decision. Sometimes, we make a decision, even if we know it's not a good idea,

especially if we feel conflicted. If it's down to social pressures, you can reassess why you made that decision and think about how you can avoid making that kind of decision in the future.

2. What options do you have? – When you make a decision, it's a good idea to consider the different solutions available to you. You wouldn't have to make a decision if you didn't have options, so brain-dump the options you have. Being able to see your options on paper can help you see your choices clearly, and therefore you can connect with the best decision.

3. What are the consequences? – Consider what the consequences might be based on the actions you take. This will help you consider the importance or seriousness of your decision. If you're unsure, ask an adult what they believe the consequences would be.

4. Is it in your best interests (or those of others)? – You need to think about the decision you have to make and consider if it's in the best interests of yourself or others to do this. If it's not, you should consider your other options and then answer question 1 – why?

5. Run your decision by others if you're feeling stuck. You could ask your family, friends, or even your teacher.

6. If you make the wrong decision, don't be too hard on yourself – of course, the aim is to make good decisions, but don't allow poor ones to deter you. This is normal, but in order to make them matter, you should learn from them. Think about how you can resolve or change the outcome, and hold yourself accountable for your actions.

It's going to happen... Once in a while, you'll make a decision that wasn't the best, but that's life; it happens. There are some things you can do to make sure that you learn from the experience because if you make a bad decision, you need to know how to rectify this yourself.

★ If you make a poor decision and feel like it makes you unsafe, you should speak to an adult as soon as possible about what happened. Even if you're worried you could get into trouble, you should still be honest. Part of growing up involves taking responsibility.

★ Remember, there are consequences for your actions. Reflect on your decision and think about the consequences you've faced because of the recent bad decision you've made. *If you had to make that same decision again:*

   o *What would you do instead?*

   o *Why?*

   o *What would you like to have happened, ideally?*

★ Stay calm and be patient. You can't look at a problem and learn from it if you're panicking. Don't blame yourself or others, either. Concentrate only on the decision and the outcome you would have preferred.

★ If you regret your decision, think about what you could do to rectify this or improve the situation. If there's nothing you can do, move on. You've learned from it already by reflecting on your decision.

★ Always talk your bad decisions over with an adult if you're worried or unsure about the outcome and need some advice or guidance.

Let's look at a scenario of a bad decision and what consequences it may result in...

Say you decided to play video games before doing your chores. You lost track of time and spent longer on that than you intended to. Mom wasn't happy because you didn't keep up with your responsibility. The consequences are:

★ You don't get your allowance until your chores are done.

★ You still have your chores to do.

★ Mom isn't happy with you because you didn't do what you were supposed to. She insists you do your chores tomorrow, or there will be further consequences.

The next day, you regret your decision because your friend wants to go to the movies that night, but now you don't have your allowance, and you can't go because you still have to do your chores. While this isn't a serious matter that leaves you unsafe, you're probably feeling really disappointed because you want to go to the movies. That's understandable, but you need to reflect on why this has happened, to ensure it doesn't happen again.

Activity #7 – Good or Bad Decision?

Making good decisions takes practice, but let's check out your perception of a bad decision. What would you do in each situation? Talk it over with a friend or adult.

Scenario - You have a test tomorrow, but your friend wants to talk on the phone. They're upset about something, but you're worried about performing well on your _test_.

1. _What are your options?_

2. _Is there a compromise to be made here?_

3. *What do you believe is a good decision?*

4. *What do you think is a bad decision?*

5. *What could be the consequences of your actions if you either don't study for your test or if you don't talk to your friend?*

6. *When you talk it over with a friend or adult, what do they suggest?*

7. *What did you learn from this?*

Now you're learning how to make good decisions; you just need to practice and reflect on the important decisions you make, and whether they're good or bad. We talked about 'responsibilities' in this chapter, and in the next chapter, we'll delve into this a little more. The focus will be on achieving your full potential by reaching for your dreams, but this also links in with your responsibilities.

It's time to dream big!

Chapter 8:

Reach for the Stars

"Don't set limits on your unlimited potential." ~ Anonymous

Fulfilling your potential and responsibilities means you can work toward being the best you can be and start striving toward your dreams, so you can live the life you want to. At your age, you're starting to take on more responsibilities, which is a big step for you as you head toward your tween or teenage years. Many tweens take responsibility for tidying their room and maybe do some chores, like washing the dishes. This is great because it helps to prepare you for teenage and adult life.

You may have big plans or dreams about what you want to do or be in the future. If you don't have plans, you may at least have some idea – but don't worry, this isn't set in stone, as it's important to accept that sometimes things change.

This chapter starts off by discussing why it's important to be responsible, and how you can work on this. We'll also talk about how you can reach your full potential and exactly what that means for you. At the end of the chapter, you'll have the opportunity to consider your future and think about what you want to do when you're older.

Before we talk about what the future holds for you, let's talk about why it's important to be responsible.

Why Is It Important to Be Responsible?

The word "responsible" is often met with an eye-roll — it's boring, *right?* The truth about responsibility is that, whether you like it or not, YOU have responsibilities, especially as you get older. Adults have a number of responsibilities, so you start with smaller responsibilities when you're younger, and as you progress in age, you take on more complex responsibilities until this becomes a normal, everyday activity that you get better at, the more practice you get.

Taking responsibility can help you:

★ Discover what you're good at and identify your strengths and weaknesses

★ Gain independence

★ Develop your ability to problem-solve

★ Manage your time better

Others aren't always going to be there to take responsibility for you. It's time to be more independent and start to do some things for yourself, as this will help you to progress. If you are responsible, you will be viewed as being more respectful, kind, and mature. It also allows you to become accountable for your actions.

Accountability goes hand-in-hand with responsibility. For example, if you're given the responsibility of chores to complete, it teaches you accountability, which means you show up and aim to achieve the things you said you would. It also encourages you to help others, as if you wash the dishes or cook a meal for the whole family, it benefits everyone.

How to Be Responsible

There are a few ways for you to begin to be more responsible. You can:

★ Set goals so you know exactly what you want to achieve.

★ Try to take a positive approach. When you're more positive, it's easier to be pro-active.

★ Avoid blaming others and focus on the things you're responsible for.

★ Accept praise graciously and allow it to motivate you.

★ Be accountable by showing up and achieving the things you say you will.

★ Prioritize what's important first and take action.

★ Take on some responsibilities, such as chores around the house.

★ Treat others with respect, honesty, and fairness.

★ Clean up after yourself without being asked.

★ Ask people to clarify if you're not sure what's expected of you.

★ Learn new skills to help you. For example, if you want to cook for your family but don't know how to cook a specific meal, ask someone to show you how.

★ Save money early on, and practice this. So many young people don't know how to manage their money well, but it's super important to learn this from a young age. Start by saving a small amount of your allowance each week – it soon mounts up.

Being responsible means you always try to respect the opinions of others, and you should ensure you listen well. A responsible person starts to take ownership of something. For example, if you tell your parents that taking the trash out is now "your" job, and you do this every week, then you're committed to doing this, and you've taken ownership.

If you want to meet your full potential in life, you need to take responsibility. It plays a huge part in doing this, but *what does fulfilling your full potential really mean for you?*

Let's talk about it...

What Does Fulfilling Your Potential Really Mean?

You have a lot of potential, and you have the right to achieve it. Sometimes, this means you have to face challenges and overcome obstacles. Reaching your full potential is a journey, it isn't a destination. It's about freeing you from the things that limit you.

Sometimes, we limit ourselves, and other times, we are limited by others. Especially when you're young, because there are rules in place that we must follow. A person who wants to reach their full potential wants to excel, which means they are motivated, driven, and focused on their goals. They are ready to do even better and keep challenging themselves. So, while they may have some idea of what they're capable of, they're ready to excel further.

If you are trying to meet your full potential, you should focus on your strengths and weaknesses. Your strengths help you identify what you are good at, while your weaknesses are simply things you need to improve. It's also important to consider activities that you enjoy doing. If you enjoy designing clothing or sportswear, for instance, you may need to practice your drawing skills in order to perfect or strengthen your designs.

A mature person knows there's always something new to learn. Reaching your potential isn't something you're going to do today, tomorrow, next week, or next year. It takes time, but that doesn't mean you shouldn't start your journey toward your full potential today.

How to Reach Your Potential

Learning this takes patience, self-awareness, and courage. These are just a few of the skills you need in order to do this effectively. Some people already believe they've reached their full potential, but this is their ego talking. As mentioned in the earlier section, there's always something else you can learn.

The truth is, if you want to reach your full potential, you need to cater to your basic needs first, as they are your foundations. For example, if you're not eating, sleeping, or drinking plenty of fluids, and fulfilling these basic needs, *how can you expect to excel at anything else?* So, if you really want to reach your potential, get the basics right first and make sure you:

★ Have a healthy diet
★ Get plenty of exercise
★ Drink plenty of fluids, and water whenever possible
★ Always get a good night's sleep
★ Have good relationships with your family, friends, and peers

These are all part of your basic needs, and it's important to get these right first.

In time, you will be able to recognize those basic needs, and you will be able to cater to them yourself. For example, you can make a drink or grab a snack. You can also take some responsibility for maintaining relationships and keeping yourself safe, at your age. The older you get, the more responsibilities you can take on, and when caring for your basic needs becomes as natural as breathing, you can move on to more complex responsibilities that will help you reach your full potential.

Are you starting to see how being responsible is linked to achieving your full potential now?

The final two key elements that will allow you to reach your full potential are:

★ Your self-esteem – which includes achievements, and respect for and from others.

★ Your self-actualization – which includes your moral compass, not judging something or someone without knowing them, acceptance, and your ability to be creative and problem-solve.

However, these are only effective if your basic needs are catered for.

Now, while this helps you understand more about how you can start to excel in life, if you really want to reach your full potential by building on your self-esteem and self-actualization, here are some top tips on how you can keep striving towards this:

★ What are your big dreams? – Know what your dreams are and create smaller steps to help you get there. For example, if you want to save $100 for a video game within one month, think about what steps you have to take to do that.

★ Embrace challenges – Taking on challenges ensures you're capable of handling the unknown and are able to problem-solve, make tough decisions, and be willing to learn.

★ Take time to reflect — Always consider *what you did, how you did it, what went well, and what requires improvement.* You should also think about anything you want to change and what could've gone better. Doing this will allow you space to grow, because there's always something to learn.

★ Be compassionate — Sometimes, things don't go as planned, so we must form a new plan. Accept that sometimes this happens. Be kind to yourself and treat this like a problem (to problem-solve), rather than a failure. *How can you overcome this?*

★ Manage your time and responsibilities — If you say you're going to do homework after school, or your chores before dinner, stick to your schedule. This shows self-discipline, and that will help you stick to deadlines in the future, as well as make sure you stay committed to your own responsibilities.

★ Self-care — Taking care of yourself is important, and this relates back to your basic needs. This is extremely important because if you're not getting good sleep, staying hydrated, and eating well, you can't function in the best possible way. Being more mindful can help you to clear your mind while staying focused on the present.

★ Take time for fun and laughter — If you want to meet your full potential, you need to enjoy your life. Spend time doing the things you enjoy doing, and make sure you take time to laugh too. While there are some things you need to take seriously, there are times when you just need fun in your life. Laughter yoga is actually a thing because it recognizes the importance of laughter when it comes to health, happiness, and well-being.

The journey to your full potential is long, but there's no reason why you can't start working toward it now. The tips provided above can help you form positive habits that you can develop now. Believe me, many adults are still trying to develop such habits today, so the earlier you begin, the better.

The stars are within your grasp!

Activity #8 – Your Potential

Complete the activities below to make a start on figuring out how you can work toward meeting your full potential. You may not know exactly what that is yet, but you have the tools to get there.

You may not want to complete all seven activities at once, but each of these things can help you as you work towards being the best you can be. Discuss them with a family member or friend, or write down your answers if you wish.

1. Name two things you're responsible for right now.
2. Name three things you could be responsible for in the near future.
3. Write yourself a goal you want to achieve within the next three months. Think about the smaller steps you may have to take to get there.
4. Name three things you're good at.
5. Name three things you need to improve.
6. How can you improve those things? What do you need to do?

7. Brain-dump your big dream – within the next 10 years, *what do you want to achieve?* Remember, this doesn't have to be set in stone. Dreams change. But right now, *what is your big dream for your future?*

It's time to move on to Chapter 9, and you're really on the home stretch with this book now. It's time to think about what makes you stand up and pay...

ATTENTION!

Chapter 9:

Pay Attention!

What makes you stand up and pay attention?

Maybe you're listening to your music and you hear your mom yell your name, or when you're asleep and the "beep" of your alarm begins to blast out like some kind of siren, or when the bell rings at school. My point is that there are many things that catch our attention, but *have you ever lost that? Have your parents or teachers ever told you that you should pay more attention?*

When I was younger, I used to wonder what the fuss was all about. *What did paying attention mean, and why did it matter so much?*

Your attention is your ability to tune in to a specific situation and often requires you to retain information by actively listening while tuning out everything else. A person's attention span is limited because you can only pay attention for a certain amount of time, so this means you must be able to pay attention at the right time, because it helps you make sense of everything.

When something or someone gets your attention, you become engaged in what's being said, and it helps you focus, process, and recall information. You may engage by asking questions and showing more of an interest in the topic.

This chapter will talk about how you can be more engaged, how you can improve your attention span, and how being more mindful can help. This will give you more of an understanding when it comes to your attention. But first, we'll talk about why paying attention is so important.

Why Is It Important to Pay Attention?

Paying attention is a valuable skill, which can make you more creative. If you can pay attention to every detail, your brain collects the information, and this provides you with a foundation for your creative ideas. Paying attention also helps improve your focus, which means you begin to notice things you did not previously notice.

Paying attention can also help you value things in life, which will make you more grateful and appreciative. It increases your knowledge and understanding of the things you're interested in and expands your perspective, which means you are able to see the bigger picture or different sides to things.

Paying more attention also helps you:

1. Make better decisions
2. Find it easier to control and manage your emotions
3. Be able to make better connections
4. Feel happier, more confident, and worthy
5. Trust yourself
6. Experience life fully
7. Stay healthy

Paying attention is one thing, but there are a few things you need to perfect, in order to increase your attention span. Let's start by talking about your memory. Having good recall skills is an excellent way to improve your attention.

Practicing Recall Skills

Your recall skills are an important part of your ability to not just pay attention, but also retain the detailed information you observe. There are some things you can do to practice these skills:

★ Look at an image for 30 seconds and try to remember as much as you can about it. Then, either write down or tell someone what you can remember from the picture.

★ Read a book or at least a chapter, and then quiz yourself on the book:

a) Write down three events from the story and put them in the order they happened.

b) Summarize what you've just read or retell the whole story if you can.

c) Write a sentence about what you think will happen next and say why you think so.

★ Get an adult to ask you about your day and answer their questions as quickly and clearly as you can.

★ Talk about an event that happened recently and tell your friends all about it. Tell them your favorite part of the event as well as your least favorite part.

★ Play a pairing game with a friend. All you need is a pack of cards. Just:

a) Lay them all face-down on a table or floor.

b) Take turns turning two over at a time.

c) The objective of the game is to find a pair (two cards) with matching numbers.

d) If your cards do not match, put them back, face down, and try to remember where they are, in case you need them to match the other cards you uncover.

e) If they match, take them and keep them in a pile. Take another turn.

f) The person with the most sets of cards at the end is the winner.

Good recall helps you learn more effectively too, and is a key part of improving your ability to pay attention. If you're going to test your mind and ability to recall, it's also good practice to take care of your mind, by embracing mindfulness.

Mindfulness Skills

Mindfulness is when you start to pay attention to your mind, body, and surroundings by focusing on the present moment, without casting judgment. Its origins stem from Buddhist practices, and it makes you more self-aware and can help you take care of your own mental well-being. Regardless of how old or young you are, mindfulness can have a positive impact on your life. Mindfulness can help improve your sleep, regulate your emotions, and improve your mood. It strengthens your self-esteem and confidence, as well as improves your focus, memory, learning, and creativity, which you need if you want to improve your attention skills.

If your muscles ache, mindfulness can also help with that, because it lowers your stress hormones and reduces tension in your muscles and joints. Many people who practice mindfulness are more empathetic and compassionate, too.

Mindfulness ultimately helps you disengage from your thoughts, which helps you to clear your busy mind. You can then relax and refresh, which then gets you ready for your day ahead. You'll find you're able to focus your attention on the task you want to complete and will be more productive.

The creative mindfulness activities below can help you relax, slow down, and de-stress. To practice mindfulness, you should:

1. Draw or color. It's a great way to distract and then clear your mind, by providing something else for you to focus on and explore your creativity.

2. Listen to music or make your own. Maybe you have a keyboard, or you could make a homemade instrument, such as a rainmaker:

   a) Seal one of the ends of a cardboard tube with scrunched-up paper and tape.

   b) Fill the cardboard tube halfway with rice,

   c) Seal the other end with paper and tape, just like you did on the first side.

   d) Now you have an instrument that sounds like rain when you tilt it from side to side.

3. Practice some relaxing breathing exercises. This is the first step towards meditation:

   a) Sit in a comfortable position in a quiet place.

   b) Keep your back straight and close your eyes.

   c) Breathe in through your nose for four seconds, hold for four seconds, and then breathe out for five.

   d) Keep your mind clear by concentrating on your breathing. To do this, you may need to count quietly to yourself, "1, 2, 3, 4," in line with your breaths.

   e) Repeat these steps about 5-10 times or until you feel relaxed.

There are endless benefits to being more mindful, but the most important one is that it can improve your mental and physical health.

The Secrets to Engaging Better

When you engage, you become involved because, ultimately, something has attracted you or caught your attention. You become involved by listening, talking, and contributing to a conversation or situation. Some young people and children don't find it easy to engage. They don't want to talk, listen, or contribute, or maybe they don't have the confidence to do so. But that's okay; engaging takes time and practice. There are some ways you can learn to engage better, and it's time you discovered the secrets.

Secret #1 – The importance of meaningful conversation

Conversation is valuable. It lets you share your opinions and feelings. Practice having conversations in which you give your time to others. You need to give each other your undivided attention, so shut off any technology and any other distractions and ask the other person to do the same. Then simply take turns talking. This could be about something specific, like something you are worried about, your day, the vacation you're going on soon, or a problem you have. Giving time to others to have conversations is the first step toward engaging better.

Secret #2 – Learn to interact appropriately

Interaction is important during conversations. You should learn to interact appropriately, which means knowing when to talk and when to listen. The more you practice interactions, the better you'll be able to read the feelings of others, which makes you even better at the way you interact. For example, if you sense someone you are close to is upset, you may show support by hugging them or by touching their arm to let them know you're there for them. You can only read emotions and feelings if you give the other person your full attention and with practice.

Secret #3 – Ask others to question you, to expand your thinking skills

When you interact, get others to challenge you by asking you complex and open-ended questions. Being asked "what" and "why" questions is a good start, as they often require more than a one-word answer, so you are pushed to think of a more detailed response. You should think of questions to ask them, too. This broadens your thinking because it gives you the bigger picture and helps you understand different perspectives.

Secret #4 – Speak from the heart

If you're trying to engage better, the best thing you can do is to be honest and kind, but also speak from the heart. Don't be afraid to show your emotions; for example, if a friend tells you something sad, show that you're sad. If they tell you something bad, show that you're angry, frustrated or upset, and if it's something that makes you happy, show joy and celebrate together. We talked about regulating your emotions in Chapter 3 of this book, so head back there if you need to clarify the principles we discussed earlier. The more emotions you show when having a conversation, the more likely people are to open up to you, and your ability to engage with others will improve.

Secret #5 – Find common ground

A good way to engage with others better is to find something you both have in common. Maybe you have a sibling, and you both enjoy playing video games or football (or another sport), or maybe you both like art or crafts of some sort. Having something in common or taking part in a hobby together can help to build relationships, and will provide more opportunities for you to develop your engagement skills. Finding something in common gives you something to talk about, and because you're interested, you'll practice your engagement skills more often.

Steps for Improving Your Attention Span

As well as improving your recall skills, embracing mindfulness, and developing your ability to engage, there are some other steps you can take to improve your attention span.

1. Do 20-30 minutes of physical exercise first thing in the morning.
2. Take an attention break that allows you to refresh – taking a drink of water or going for a walk are great ways to do this. Taking breaks helps you refocus.
3. Remove visual distractions – it's a good idea to remove clutter, or any type of technology, such as iPads or cell phones, so you have no excuses.
4. Play games that test your memory – we talked about the "pairs" card game earlier in this chapter, but you can also try I Spy or Simon Says.
5. If you have a task to do that's complicated or is going to take a long time, break it down into small steps. That way, you can tick off the steps you complete and monitor your progress.

Activity #9 – Practicing Mindfulness to Increase Your Focus

There are many different mindful activities you can do to help you refocus and increase your attention span (along with many other benefits). The activity below is really useful:

1. Find somewhere quiet and comfortable where you won't be disturbed.
2. Either sit or lie down.
3. Take some deep relaxing breaths. In through the nose for four seconds, hold for four seconds, and out through the mouth for five seconds. Repeat three times.
4. Close your eyes and focus on each sense in turn:
   a) What can you smell?
   b) What can you taste?
   c) What can you feel?
   d) What can you hear?
   e) Now, open your eyes. What can you see?
5. Wiggle your fingers and toes, and when you're ready, stand up.
6. Stretch your arms up above your head and breathe in.
7. Breathe out and push your arms out to the side and down until they're by your sides.
8. Finally, either write about or draw a picture that represents your senses today.

Remember, developing your attention skills is not something you can do quickly and easily. It takes time and patience. These skills will benefit you as you head into your teens and later into your adulthood, so if you master them now, you'll be an expert by then. In the next chapter, it's time to say please, as we focus on good manners and empathy, which are extremely important social skills to embrace.

Chapter 10:

Empathy and Good Manners

Do your parents often tell you to "use your manners" when speaking to others?

Or maybe they tell you, *"Don't say anything at all if you can't say anything nice."*

In this chapter, we're going to focus on empathy and good manners. We'll discuss what empathy is and how you can use it. We'll also learn what it means to have good manners and how they can help you succeed in life.

Before we make a start, let's look at the quote below:

"It's nice to be important, but it's more important to be nice."
~ Author Unknown

What Is Empathy?

Empathy is when you can put yourself in another person's shoes and understand how they might feel in any situation. You can imagine this thing happening to you, and therefore, you know what you would be feeling in their place.

For example, if a friend of yours falls over and cuts their knee, and they are hurt, you understand that because something similar has happened to you before. Therefore, you are able to respond in an appropriate way. You wouldn't just say, "Be tough and get up," because you would be aware of their pain.

It's the same with name-calling. Let's say that someone has called another person a horrible name, and as a result, that person is crying. You know the name is awful, so you put yourself in the other person's shoes, and therefore you make sure they're okay. You may even stand up for them.

Empathy; Why Do We Need It and How Do We Develop It?

You're probably wondering why we need empathy. People who have empathy are able to build good relationships with others because they develop a caring nature, as they can imagine how other people feel. It's so much more than simply being "nice" – it helps you be a good person and learner.

People who are more empathetic are able to develop their emotional intelligence. This is basically the ability to manage your own emotions and manage them well. This means you have better health and well-being as a result since you can understand and explain to others how you feel. Showing empathy can also help you learn. When we study, we have to be able to consider what the text is telling us, and empathy helps us to understand what it means by the feeling it evokes. It also aids group work, as it ensures you understand why we must take turns. If someone isn't getting a turn in the group and you empathize, you'll know how they feel, and therefore, you can try to make sure they're involved.

In a world of bullying (including cyber), empathy is crucial, as it helps you to consider how others feel, both in person and online. It can build tolerance of others and even prevent bullying. The thing is, empathy doesn't come easy. It's something you have to work on and practice (like most of the skills we've discussed so far in this book).

Think about how others, such as your friends, parents, family, or teachers, empathize with you when you're having a tough time.

It's good to learn empathy from others, so think about what they do when you're feeling sad or upset. *Do they try to understand you and show you compassion?*

You can develop your empathy every day. In fact, you've probably already made a start, but here are some ideas to help you get started:

1. Practice being kind at least once per day. A random act of kindness can go a long way. Although kindness and empathy are different, make it your mission to be kind every day of your life.

2. Learn more about emotions and build your vocabulary around this. It can be difficult to identify, manage, and understand your emotions, so keep working on this. If you can't identify your emotions, talk to an adult and ask them to help you identify and name them, by telling them about what caused this feeling to occur.

3. Read a book. Reading storybooks teaches us empathy because they introduce us to many fictional scenarios and there are always lessons to be learned. An avid reader certainly has the opportunity to improve and strengthen their empathy.

4. If you encounter unkindness or do something unkind, explore where it came from. If a friend does something and you say something unkind to them, try to talk it over with an adult and consider why you said it and why it wasn't acceptable. This is not about you being in trouble, so ask your parent to help you come up with a solution – *what should you have done instead?*

5. Limit your screen time. Screen time is not good for you and can impact your mood and mental health. Limiting your screen time can help improve your empathy skills, as it's likely you'll have more opportunities to interact with others, socialize, and play. Give it a try!

What Are Good Manners?

Good manners tell other people a lot about you. They are often expected by adults, as they show respect and maturity. Manners are a standard that we are taught to live by, as they teach us how we need to act in specific social situations. If you practice good manners, you'll have a better attitude, be more optimistic, and you'll have charisma, which means your personality will be attractive, and people may even look up to you.

Manners are shown in your behavior. You could:

★ Say "please" and "thank you"
★ Hold the door open for someone
★ Not interrupt or talk over people
★ Be honest and always avoid lying
★ Wait your turn patiently in line

How Can Good Manners Help You Succeed in Life?

Manners can help you succeed in life because they are a positive attribute that shows respect and maturity. If you are polite and considerate to others, it shows you care, and others will find it easy to talk to you. Children who learn and develop their manners from a young age are much more socially attentive throughout their teenage and adult years.

Having good manners helps to build positive relationships with others, including your family, friends, neighbors, teachers, and others. It can also enhance your self-esteem and confidence, which helps to develop your other social skills and boost your ability to communicate. Saying please and thank you goes a long way, but manners are so much more than that, because when we meet a person who has good manners, we remember them, and we know it's likely they are genuinely nice human beings. Having good manners ultimately leads to your success!

Let's not forget this book is all about social skills, and having good manners helps with that too. If you demonstrate good manners, people are more likely to listen to you, cooperate with you, be friends with you, and respect you. Good manners show you have morals, and by practicing them daily, you're showing you're committed to them. Having good manners says a lot about your personality too, as it shows you in a positive light. Manners are always appreciated.

We usually learn good manners from the people in our lives who influence us, such as our parents and teachers. If you want to develop your manners, it's a good idea to think of a person you know who has good manners, shows kindness, and is generous, and observe how they behave. Practicing being polite and well-mannered can open up opportunities for you in the future.

Activity #10 – Big "Talk" (Empathy Scenario and Good Manners)
For this activity, you need the help of an adult. Look at the scenario below and discuss how you could respond empathetically.

You have a science test coming up at school next week. You call your friend for a chat, and they're very quiet. You ask what's wrong, and they tell you that in the practice test, they got a much lower grade than they expected. They don't know where they went wrong, but they tell you they're worried about the upcoming test and start to cry. *

1. What would you say, and how would you show empathy?
2. Ask an adult to give you feedback on your answer.

Having good manners goes hand-in-hand with empathy. They are both equally important building blocks to help you develop your social skills while also building positive relationships.

We're going to talk about respecting boundaries next, which goes together with manners and empathy and is also a very important social skill. It's important to respect other's boundaries, but also to have the confidence to set your own. Many young people feel pressured into doing things they're uncomfortable with, because they don't know how to let others know their boundaries, or maybe they don't know what their boundaries are exactly.

Let's get clear and comfortable with boundaries!

PERSONAL SPACE

Chapter 11:

Respecting Boundaries

Do you find it easy or difficult to say no?

Many people find it difficult to say no from time to time, and this isn't simply referring to children and young people, because adults can find it just as difficult.

What about if you encounter a situation that makes you uncomfortable? What do you do or say?

The reason I'm asking you is that saying no or expressing how you feel about a particularly uncomfortable situation isn't always easy. It may not be easy for your friends either, which is why we're discussing boundaries in this chapter, so you can learn how and why to respect the boundaries of others, and how to set your own boundaries, too.

Boundaries are important as they show that you respect another person and that they respect you, too. They are healthy and demonstrate knowledge of personal space. We'll also provide you with some assertiveness skills, so you can feel more comfortable saying no.

It's not uncommon for us to do something we know is wrong or don't want to do, due to feeling pressured by others, which can include pressure from friends. This pressure isn't always intentional, but it can be difficult to deal with, so in this chapter, we'll also cover peer pressure and consider how you should respond to it.

We'll make a start by learning more about boundaries...

Know Your Own Boundaries

Your parents or other adults in your family will have set rules for you to follow. Maybe you have to be home for dinner, or maybe you can only play with friends once your homework is completed. These are boundaries you have to live by. Boundaries will be set at school, too. For example, your teacher may have rules of no shouting in class, no cell phones, and they could set rules about being kind to one another. Boundaries are very similar to rules because a boundary is a limit or an imaginary line that you shouldn't cross.

You could have that favorite outfit in your closet, and while you don't mind your siblings borrowing your clothes if they ask first, your boundary is that they don't touch your favorite outfit – it's your limit.

We all have limits. Your parents set boundaries for you when you're young, and this is to give you a nudge in the right direction when it comes to your behavior and the things you should or shouldn't do. So take a moment and visualize the different boundaries you have...

Many people also have body-related and personal boundaries, which we'll discuss next.

When you set boundaries, it's important that you demand respect for them. This means you must communicate them to others effectively, by using the right tone. Being firm but friendly is the best way to do this. It can be difficult to be firm, so that's why we're covering assertiveness later in this chapter. You also need to be consistent. So, if someone keeps borrowing your things without asking, keep letting them know you don't like it and tell them about your boundaries and expectations again. It's also good to have some patience, too. When you first set new boundaries, it can take others some time to get used to them, but consistency is the key to demanding that your boundaries be respected.

Let's move on now and talk about body boundaries.

Body Boundaries and Personal Space

We all have boundaries regarding our bodies and personal space. This is a good thing. When we have our own personal space, we feel comfortable. If others invade our personal space, we can feel uncomfortable or threatened.

When it comes to personal space, there are not any guidelines on how much space you need, but this is a boundary you can set, based on what you feel is appropriate. The amount of personal space a person needs is different for everyone, and it's likely the space you need depends on some key things, such as:

★ What you are doing

★ Where you are

★ Who you are with

It's likely that if you are upset, your personal space requirements will be smaller for a family member than for your teacher or neighbor, but only you can set these boundaries!

If you're struggling to determine your personal space, don't be afraid to let others know. Ask for advice from a family member or friend and ask them what they feel is appropriate.

If someone invades your personal space and you feel uncomfortable, you should stay calm, then let them know in a clear but polite way. For example, it's okay to:

★ Say, "Could you please back up? You're in my personal space."

★ Say, "Please don't touch me/stop touching me."

★ Make a "stop" gesture with your hand.

★ Walk away.

★ Get an adult to help you.

When thinking of personal boundaries, it's good to imagine a hula hoop around your waist, and if people are outside of the hoop, they're a safe distance away from you. Your personal space keeps you safe, but sometimes, you need to allow people into the circle. Let's say you want to hug your grandparents or another family member; then they can enter that space. Of course, there are people you will want to show affection to, and that's fine. You decide who can and can't enter that space — it's up to you! You should be aware of other people's personal space boundaries, too, and not invade them unless you know they are comfortable with it.

At the age you are now (or soon), you'll get yourself dressed, and you probably do this in private, as you start to be aware of boundaries in relation to your body. Body boundaries don't happen at a set age, but it's around this time (a little earlier or later for some). It's also likely you bathe without supervision too, but your parents or other family members might check on you or ask you to leave the door unlocked as a safety precaution. This is because you are starting to develop body boundaries, and you understand that, as you head toward your teenage years, there are certain things that you want to do in private.

Why Is It Important to Respect Other People's Boundaries?

We've talked a lot about respect in this book. As you get older, social interactions get a little tricky, and having a set of rules to guide you ensures you stay on the right track. When we respect the boundaries of others, it shows that we understand their needs. When we set our own boundaries, it shows we respect our own needs. We've already talked about empathy, respect, and manners, and they're all closely linked with boundaries. Good things to remember include:

★ People are in charge of their own bodies, so respect their wishes regarding them.

★ Listen when others are giving instructions, expressing how they feel, or asking you to do something,

★ What seems like fun for you may not be fun for someone else, so it's always good to make sure.

Other people must respect your boundaries like you respect theirs. Respecting boundaries is another way to strengthen the relationships in your life, and they should always be taken seriously. It can also strengthen your ability to empathize. Everyone is different, so it's important to use your empathy by putting yourself in the shoes of the other person and ensuring you respect their boundaries. Setting boundaries also helps reduce conflict, as it encourages you to keep communication channels open with others. Having a range of healthy boundaries of your own also influences your behavior for the better.

What Is Peer Pressure, and How Should You Respond to It?

Peer pressure is when a person or group of people makes you feel like you need to do something, even if you don't want to do it. It's quite common for the people around us to have an influence on what we do or how we do something. However, we should never feel forced or pressured.

Let's say your friend decides not to go to school today, and they keep asking you not to go either, and to stay with them. That means pretending you've left for school and lying to your parents, because they'll believe you've gone to school. You don't want to do it, but you also don't want to let your friend down. They're saying things to you such as, "Nobody will know," "Please, I don't want to be alone," or "Go on, don't be a chicken," but all of this persuasive language is putting pressure on you to do something you don't want to do and know you shouldn't be doing.

We all want to make and keep friends, so sometimes it can be difficult to say no, as you want to make your friends happy. Just because it makes them happy doesn't mean you should do it. The truth is, a true friend wouldn't ask you to do something that makes you unhappy.

When dealing with peer pressure, it's important to remember:

★ You have the power to make your own choices, so you should. Don't let others have too much of an influence if you know it's wrong – you're responsible!

★ Saying no is okay, especially if you don't feel comfortable or safe. Be assertive and say it with confidence. Practice this if you need to.

★ You will still be accepted, even if you say no. You can tell them you can't, don't want to, or it isn't a good idea. A true friend will accept your decision.

★ You can choose friends who share the same values and interests as you, so you don't find yourself in difficult or uncomfortable situations.

★ Make another suggestion. Let's say you don't want to miss school; tell them you'll catch up with them after school instead.

★ When you feel confident, try to speak up for others if you notice they are being pressured into doing something they don't want to do.

★ Sometimes, you just need to avoid these situations. For example, if you know in advance your friend is going to miss school, don't walk to school with them that day.

★ While you're already good at making decisions, you can always ask an adult to help you make a good decision if you're unsure.

Sometimes, you must be assertive!

Being Assertive – Five Top Tips

Being assertive takes confidence. A person is usually confident when they take care of themselves and when they are able to communicate effectively. Developing the life skills you've learned (and are about to learn) in this book can help you become more assertive, but like every skill, it still takes practice.

1. Don't confuse assertiveness with anger – when you're assertive, you're calm and wise, but firm.

2. Put clear boundaries in place and communicate them well.

3. Use "I" messages when explaining how you feel to others, as this prevents blaming others, and can reduce conflict. For example: "I feel like this when you behave like that." You can even tell the person what you want them to do, following this with, "I would like you to stop/another request."

4. Develop your friendship skills. We talked about choosing friends earlier in this book, and assertiveness skills can be developed through your ability to make, choose, and maintain friends. Some people, such as those who bully you or make you feel bad about yourself, are not really your friends. Discussing topics regarding friendships and choosing friends (and considering how a good friend acts) can enhance your

assertiveness skills. It helps you identify your expectations for a good friend, and who would make a bad friend.

5. Watch others who are confident and enlist the help of an adult. The best way to build confidence is to watch how others communicate confidently and learn from this. Think about how your parents and teachers deal with specific situations. For example, they say "no" with confidence, and their tone shows they mean it. They are also calm when they communicate, so by enlisting their help, you can practice, they can praise you or provide feedback, and you can discuss the difficulties you have with being assertive so they can give you advice.

Developing your assertiveness skills takes time, so be patient with yourself. Set small goals to help you improve your assertiveness.

Activity #11 – Set Your Boundaries

You've been thinking about boundaries, which is great, but it's time to put this into practice.

1. Think of 3-5 boundaries that are important to you – write them down.

2. Share your boundaries with a parent or other family member.

3. Practice being assertive. Imagine the person has broken one of your boundaries and deal with them using your assertiveness skills.

This chapter has been amazing as we have discussed the importance of boundaries, personal space, peer pressure, and assertiveness. In the final chapter, we're going to focus on all things positive, because happiness is important too!

Chapter 12:

Staying Positive, Being Kind, and Embracing Happiness

"Being happy never goes out of style."
—Lilly Pulitzer, Fashion Designer

You've made it to the final chapter, which means you're embracing your social skills. It's important we finish this book with lots of positives, because as the quote suggests above, being happy is a very good thing.

In this chapter, you will focus on being happy, positive, and kind, and consider how this can be beneficial. You'll explore how to embrace positivity, even if things aren't going your way. Sometimes, things don't go as planned and it can impact our mood and how we feel. Adopting a positive outlook, being kind, and choosing to be happy is a great mindset to adopt for your future growth and development – let's always be looking on the bright side of life.

Some of the skills you've already learned in this book can contribute to your mindset, so we'll briefly touch on those as we discuss how you can be positive, embrace happiness, and act in a kind way, while also exploring the benefits in this short and snappy final chapter.

What Are the Benefits of Being Positive, Kind, and Happy?

There are many benefits to being positive, kind, and happy. It can improve how you feel, both physically and mentally, and leave you feeling great. It can also help you cope better, especially when you're faced with difficult situations and at times of stress.

When you're happy, it impacts your body in a positive way, and this may also impact others – they may feel better because of how you're behaving. This boosts your mood and encourages you to feel fulfillment and joy. It can also help you strengthen relationships because it's easier to be friends and connect with someone who is positive, happy, and kind, since they make us feel great too.

Adopting a positive mindset means that you regularly respond to situations in a positive and kind way. It means you put things into perspective and look at them logically. By staying calm, not overreacting, and using both your problem-solving skills and empathy to deal with the situation, you can still remain positive, even during the tough times you face in your life.

It can take practice if you want to adopt such a positive mindset. Being kind shows that you think of others. Also, a person who is happier is often more productive, healthier, has a better immune system, and is willing to do things for or give to others.

If you maintain a positive mindset, happiness can be a choice. This doesn't mean you won't be sad, angry, or frustrated at times. It simply means you choose happiness as often as you possibly can and don't allow your other emotions to overwhelm you or take over.

Let's choose happiness!

How to Be Positive

The first step to choosing happiness is adopting a positive mindset. This takes practice and can be easier said than done, but having a positive attitude can really help you overcome the problems you encounter in life because it makes you resilient. To develop your positivity, the first step is to learn how to manage your emotions better. You already have the skills to do this, as we learned in Chapter 3, so you're well on your way to developing a positive mindset.

The second step involves improving your attitude, and you can do that by being open to humor. It's also a good idea to surround yourself with positive people, as those with a negative attitude (when people are not helpful, do not believe good things happen, and are uncooperative) can bring you down with them.

It isn't always easy to stay positive, so reward yourself for doing so. This doesn't have to be with anything expensive. Maybe you deserve to take some time to do things you enjoy, such as playing online games, watching television, cooking, or hanging out with friends. This will help you stay motivated!

How to Embrace Happiness

Happiness is reflective of your mood and state of mind. We are typically happy when everything is going right for us; for example, when life is good, and the relationships we have are all going well. It's important to remember, though, that nobody is always happy.

There are lots of ways you can embrace happiness, and we've already discussed several of them in this book. Here is a reminder, in case you want to head back to the relevant chapter and take a look:

★ Be grateful for the things you have and practice gratitude daily
★ Practice mindfulness
★ Get plenty of sleep and allow yourself time to rest and relax

★ Work on positive relationships, including the friendships in your life

★ Get moving – this could mean going for a walk, or other forms of exercise

★ Don't hold grudges – be forgiving of others

★ When you encounter a problem, work on solving it rather than dwelling on it

★ Be kind to yourself

★ If you use social media, take a break from it

★ Sunshine is another thing that can make you happy. There's nothing better than feeling the warm glow of the sun on your face!

There is a range of other things that can make us happy, and these will differ from one person to the next. With this in mind, you should consider doing something that makes you happy every day.

You deserve it!

Acts of Kindness

We sometimes encounter unkindness in our lives, and it's never a pleasant experience. If you've ever encountered a bully, have been subjected to online nastiness, or simply just run into someone who was mean to you, you'll understand the impact of this.

It should be a goal of yours to be kind because it's the right thing to do. It's never necessary to be unkind, and there are no rewards for this, but when you are kind, there are many rewards. People will like you and feel able to connect with you, which will strengthen relationships you have. You'll also gain a reputation for being a good-natured and kind person, and let's face it, we need more kindness in the world.

To be kind, you could:

1. Volunteer to help with a charity event
2. Do a good deed
3. Compliment someone
4. Be kind to yourself – do something for you
5. Let someone borrow something of yours
6. Help a friend with their homework
7. Help your parents or other family members with chores, like the laundry

There are all sorts of different ways to be kind, and a simple act of kindness can make someone else's day.

Activity #12 – Seven Acts of Kindness

It's time to build kindness into your daily life.

1. Take a moment and think about the kind things you can do over the next week.
2. Create a brain-dump by putting all your kindness ideas onto a piece of paper.
3. Choose seven acts of kindness you can do over the next week.
4. As you complete each of these acts, check them off.
5. If you complete all seven within seven days, reward yourself.

Conclusion

The Social Skills for Amazing Kids book was designed to help you develop your social skills so you're able to improve friendships, communicate how you feel, set boundaries, and improve your attention skills, but it's so much more than that.

You've learned about the importance of social skills in your life, and now you have an understanding of how they can enrich it. You've also considered how you can improve your communication skills through body language and other non-verbal cues, as well as gaining a deeper understanding of active listening and its importance.

Probably the most important life skill you'll learn in this book is identifying, dealing with, and regulating your emotions, which can be a difficult thing at your age. Your emotions and communication skills are keystones when it comes to developing your other social skills.

Making friends is important for you at this age, but friendships tend to be much more complex. That's why you've learned how to make friends and keep them, how to be a good friend, how to choose friends, and how to manage conflict. Even the best friendships sometimes encounter conflict, so it's a really good idea to learn how to deal with such issues.

Other important life skills you've learned in this book are problem-solving, negotiation skills, decision-making, taking on responsibilities, reaching your potential, and improving your attention. All these things will help you grow personally and in your education. If you master these skills, you may start to notice your grades improve, as well as your attitude and motivation. This book also looked at good manners and empathy, respect, boundaries, peer pressure, and how to embrace happiness. It focused on helping you to develop a positive mindset, which will ensure you are motivated, happy, and productive in everything you do. You'll learn to build kindness into your daily life because kindness helps you to keep growing into a helpful, morally-sound person who considers others and values themselves. A bit more kindness never hurt anyone, so be sure to make an extra effort to develop your emotional intelligence.

If you practice and master the social skills in this book, there's no doubt that you'll become a happy, grateful, and confident young person as you move forward into your tween or teenage years, but the skills you've learned will also take you into adulthood.

You've got it all figured out, right? Because social skills are for life!

Now it's time to celebrate. You got through this part of the book because you're the coolest tween on the planet, but *how are you going to reward yourself for this achievement?*

Only you can decide…

Social Dilemmas

60 Common Social Dilemmas Faced by Tweens

Congratulations on finishing the first part of the book! You can now apply your newfound knowledge to handle sixty various social situations that you or those around you might encounter. Let's observe how you navigate each scenario.

They are divided into the following categories:

Self Regulation

Social Consciousness

Building Relationships

Personal Development

Self-Regulation

Self-regulation refers to how you manage your feelings, behaviors, and thoughts in various situations.

1. **Communicating Emotions**

   It's your first day at school, and you feel a little nervous. Your mom asks you how you're feeling.

   How could you communicate how you feel?

   What do you think your mother will tell you to make you feel better?

   Hint: Some people bottle up how they feel, but it's important to learn how to express yourself.

2. **Facing the Consequences**

   You go to the mall with your friends for the first time. Even though your parents told you that you must stay in the mall itself, your friends want to go to the arcade, which is 10 minutes away. You agree, even though you know you shouldn't, as it's breaking the rules your parents have set out.

   Your parents find out and are very disappointed. They say you've broken their trust, and there will be consequences.

   What would you do?

   What do you think the consequences will be for your actions?

   How will you earn back their trust?

3. Being a Good Friend

You've told one of your friends you'll go to the movies with them, but your other friend calls you and they seem really upset. You ask them what's wrong, and they start to cry. They tell you they've had some really bad family news that they'd prefer to tell you in person, but they cannot go to the movies.

How do you think you can be a good friend to **both** friends?

Remember, there isn't always a simple answer, but to be a good friend, you have to consider honesty, keeping your word, as well as being there for your friends when you can.

4. Doing the Right Thing

You have a new teacher today, and some of your classmates are planning to play a trick on him to cause confusion. They all switch names and want you to do the same, so when attendance is called, you all answer under the wrong name. You don't think it's a good idea, but your friend tells you it's "just a joke" and you'll be the only person in the class not participating.

How do you think the joke would make your new teacher feel?

Do you think this behavior is acceptable?

What would you do?

5. Understanding Limitations

You won a competition at school, and you've been told you can collect your prize from Mrs. Bunting at the end of the school day on Friday. You head to her classroom, but it's locked, and all the lights are out. The teacher in the next classroom tells you that Mrs. Bunting had to leave in a hurry because she had an emergency at home. You've really been looking forward to receiving your prize, but the other teacher tells you you'll have to wait until Monday. You feel frustrated.

How would you deal with these feelings of frustration?

6. That's Not Fair

A kid from your class runs past you in the school parking lot and throws an egg at a teacher's car. The egg smashes, making a mess, and the teacher thinks it's you as you are the only person they can see.

You explain what happened and that it wasn't you, but they don't believe you and want to call your parents.

How would you handle this situation?

What do you think the person who threw the egg should do?

Hint: Things that happen to us in life aren't always fair, as sometimes people get it wrong.

7. Accidents Happen

A parcel is delivered to your home, but it's quite large. You manage to get it in the door, but as you turn, you knock over the table with your mom's favorite vase. It doesn't completely shatter, but there's a chip and a large crack.

What would you do in this situation?

Hint: Even though it's difficult, the truth is very important.

8. Forgive and Move On

Your sister borrowed your bicycle and fell off, damaging the bike. She injured her knee. You use your bike regularly, and you never agreed she could use it. You're angry that it's damaged.

How do you handle the situation?

What will it take for you to forgive her?

What will it take for you to move past it and let go of your grudge?

9. Respecting Boundaries

You're a hugger! You like to greet your friends with a hug, but one of your friends recently told you she doesn't like hugs and would prefer it if you didn't hug her unless she asks you to. Nobody has ever asked you to "not" hug them before, but she's explained it makes her uncomfortable.

How would you handle this situation?

What could you do to ensure you respect her request?

10. Joining In

You're at the beach with your friends. There's a volleyball net free and your friends start playing. You've never played before, but it looks fun. Your friends encourage you to join in, but you're not sure of the rules.

What would you do?

Hint: Part of growing up means trying new things and having fun with your friends. You don't always have to be so serious!

11. Dealing With Sadness

Your best friend has moved to another country, and it's your first day at school without them. Last night you felt really emotional, and as you head to school today, you feel so lonely.

You tried to call your friend yesterday, but you couldn't get an answer and still haven't heard back from them.

How do you get through the day at school?

Who can you talk to about the sadness you're feeling?

Hint: You shouldn't bottle up your feelings, especially if you're feeling sad or angry.

12. Gaming Awareness

You've been playing a video game on your game console. Your parents limit your screen time, but when they think you're in bed at night, you've been playing.

You've been staying up until the early hours, and as a result, you're tired during the day, and you're struggling to get up in time for school. You're even dreaming about the game, and last night, you were so angry because you didn't succeed, and it took you ages to switch off and go to sleep. You can't help yourself at night and feel like you have to play the game, but you know it's affecting you.

What do you think you should do?

Who can you talk to about this?

Hint: Sometimes, if you know something is wrong, you just have to own up and talk about it. It's a good idea to speak to your parents, even though you may be in trouble, they can help you.

13. The Right Style

Your parents usually buy your clothes, but you're starting to develop your own style. You want to start choosing your own clothes.

How would you explain to your parents that you want to start choosing some of your clothes?

If you can't agree on a style, can you come to a compromise?

14. Cleanliness Habits

You've been learning about personal hygiene in school, and you've been developing cleanliness habits. Your parents have always told you to get washed in the morning, and although you showered last night, you were running late this morning, so you just put on your clothes and left for school.

Your friend tells you in the politest and most private way possible that you don't smell fresh, and this isn't the first time.

Do you think it was wrong for your friend to tell you that?

What can you do to improve this?

15. Setting Your Own Boundaries

You went to the bathroom and left your bag with your friend. When you're in class later, you look for your favorite pen, but it's not there. When you look across the room, you see that your friend is using your pen.

You confront them after class, and they explain they didn't have a pen and needed to borrow one. You're not happy that they didn't ask, as that pen is valuable to you. While you would've let them borrow a pen, you wouldn't have allowed them to use the one they took.

How do you approach the situation with your friend?

How can you tell them it's not acceptable to take your things without asking?

Social Consciousness refers to the world, society, and the understanding and empathy you show regarding this.

16. Overcoming Embarrassment

It's the end of the school day. You run to meet your friends because you have something exciting to tell them, but you slip and fall over. Everyone laughs – it feels like even your friends are laughing too.

Think about how you could deal with the situation…

What would you say?

What would you do?

What would you tell yourself?

Hint: While things can sometimes happen that are really embarrassing, it often doesn't last long.

17. How Do THEY Feel?

You invite five of your friends to an amusement park over the weekend. One of your friends responds and tells you that they'd love to go; however, they just don't have the money. They want you to keep their reason for not going private.

You've never really thought about money differences between you and your friends.

Why do you think they want you to keep this a secret?

Put yourself in their shoes – how difficult do you think it was for your friend to let you know the reason they're unable to come?

18. Dealing With Difficult Situations

All your friends are invited to a birthday party, but you're not invited. You are not really friends with the person who is having the party, yet you still feel disappointed.

What can you do to help yourself feel better?

Remember, inviting everyone to your birthday party isn't always possible, so don't take it personally.

19. Standing Up for What You Believe in

You're with three of your friends at the mall, and they start talking about another friend and how she couldn't come today due to her family's financial situation.

On the way home, the conversation gets worse, and they start to say bad things about how she looks and how her home looks. This is making you feel uncomfortable, and you really wish you'd stuck up for your friend earlier at the mall.

How could you handle this situation?

How would you explain what you believe or think to your friends?

20. Making a Contribution

Your neighbor is struggling to pull out his trash can. You've known him for a few years, and he's a lovely elderly man.

How can you help him?

Why is it important to be a good neighbor?

How do you think being a good neighbor contributes to society?

21. Dealing With Bullies

One of your classmates is being bullied by some of the other students in your class. You really want to speak up about it, but you don't want to make the situation worse, and you're afraid of something happening to you.

Who could you talk to about this?

How could you handle this situation while also keeping yourself safe?

Hint: If nobody speaks out, the bully or bullies will not face the consequences of their actions.

22. Dealing With Gossip

Something happened over the summer break, but you didn't really want anyone to know about it. When you get back to school, there are rumors flying around about you, but they're only partially true, and now, everyone, except for your best friend, is treating you differently.

How can you handle this situation?

23. Kindness to Others

A classmate always brings their lunch to school, but her water bottle leaked inside her bag and ruined her lunch. At lunchtime, you notice her sitting alone, and when you talk to her, you find out she has nothing left to eat.

What would you do to help her?

Hint: If you are unable to help directly, think about who else may be able to help.

24. Being Culture Aware

Your family is very religious, but many of your friends' families are not. They don't understand why you have certain religious commitments, and this makes it difficult for you to connect with them.

How does this make you feel?

What can you do to connect with your classmates in different ways?

Is there any way to explain more about your culture to your classmates?

Remember, sometimes people don't understand things because they don't know about them. It can be up to us to educate them.

25. Understanding and Respecting Others' Circumstances

There's a kid down the street who is slightly younger than you, and you sometimes talk to them. They are from a large family and always comment on how nice your clothes are. You have some clothes you want to donate and want to ask them if they would like to have a look first, but you're not sure what to say.

How would you ask them in a dignified way?

Hint: Think about how you can deliver the message indirectly.

26. Having Morals and Doing the Right Thing

You're in the local store, and the person in front of you is waiting to be served. They pull out their money, and you notice $20 fall out of their pocket and onto the floor. They haven't noticed.

What do you think is the right thing to do?

27. Showing Kindness

You're sitting on the porch, and a little boy rides past your house on his bicycle. As he turns around, his wheel gets stuck, and he falls off. You ask him if he's okay, and he says he is, but his bicycle is broken. He tries to push it home, but he's struggling.

Would you help him?

If so, what would you do?

28. "Cool Kid" Language

A couple of your friends have started using foul language and words you know your parents would disapprove of. They start hassling you because you're not doing it too – you're not a cool kid if you don't use those words.

Do you think that's true?

How does this make you feel?

What would you do?

Hint: It's always helpful to think about the consequences if you're caught, and also the purpose — what is the purpose of using language like that?

29. Screen Time Limits

Your parents have set screen time limits and you think it's unfair. Your friend is allowed to watch TV late at night and always teases you because they watch things you're not allowed to watch.

You've noticed that lately, their grades are slipping and yesterday, they were so tired they fell asleep in class, and your teacher called their parents to discuss the recent issues.

Why do you think screen time limits are set?

How do you think excessive screen time can impact you?

30. Protecting Friends

Your best friend and a couple of other friends are called into the principal's office to talk about who started a fight that they witnessed. You didn't see the fight yourself. However, your best friend has told you that her friend started it, but they've lied and said it was the other person.

That means the other person is now blamed for starting the fight and could even be suspended from school. You don't really like the kid who is being blamed, but you feel uncomfortable about the situation.

Who could you talk to about this?

How could you handle this situation?

What would you do?

Hint: Sometimes, we face really difficult situations in life, and we feel torn between doing the right thing or protecting our friends and family.

Building relationships refers to how you work with others while forming healthy relationships with various people in your life, including family, friends, and neighbors.

31. Making New Friends

You have changed schools; today is your first day at your new school.

How would you try to make friends?

What information would you share about yourself?

Hint: Keep in mind the different environments you find yourself in. Whom are you sitting next to in class? Who is your lab partner? Who comes over to you in the yard at breaktime and lunchtime? Who do you live nearby?

32. Being Thankful

You're going to be late for school, as you've slept in. Your neighbor, who you know well and is a family friend, is leaving their house as you rush out the door. Your parents are at work. Your neighbor offers you a ride as they pass your school on the way to work. You accept the ride and text your parents to let them know.

You are really grateful for your neighbor's help, but how do you let them know?

Hint: Manners are important here, but what else could you do?

33. What's the Bigger Picture?

Something has been different with your friend lately, and you can't put your finger on what it is. You speak to him on the way home from school, and he tells you there are numerous things getting him down. His parents have separated, and he's had difficulties with another boy at school.

Your friend asks you to keep it a secret, and you've always been a loyal friend. But there's something not quite right, and you're worried about your friend.

How could you handle this situation?

How could you support your friend?

Hint: Supporting your friend is extremely important, but if you have a gut feeling that something horrible may happen, it's sometimes necessary to act on this.

34. Encouraging Inclusivity

There's a new student in your class and they're really quiet. This is their first week, and they don't seem to be making friends. Your friends want to hang out over the weekend, and you're discussing the different things you can do. You suggest inviting the new kid along as they live in your neighborhood, but one of your friends isn't keen on the idea – they say they like your friendship group how it is.

How would you reassure your friend that it's good to include others?

What could you do to encourage inclusivity?

35. Being a "Cheer" Leader

You and your friend used to play basketball together, but this year they made the school team, and you didn't. You can still go to practice, and while you're happy for your friend, you're feeling disappointed.

How do you think your friend feels about this?

What could you do or say to support and encourage your friend?

36. Friend or Frenemy?

You got some new sneakers over the weekend, and you told your friend. They turn up at school with the more expensive version and show your friendship group. You've been so happy as you've wanted these sneakers for a while, but because your friend has better ones, you don't have the confidence to share them.

This isn't the first time your friend has done this. She upstaged you when you got a new coat, and when you went swimming a few weeks ago, she told everyone she was getting a brand-new heated swimming pool installed in her yard.

You're starting to question your friendship...

Do you think this person is a true friend?

Why?

37. Having Difficult Conversations

One of your closest friends wants to perform in a local talent show with you, but you've done the same singing act together for the last two years. You've already asked two other classmates to perform a dance routine with you, and your first meet-up is today. Your close friend doesn't dance, and while you don't want to let them down, you really want to do something different.

How would you handle this situation?

How can you communicate this to your friend without risking your friendship?

38. Negotiation

You've been assigned a lab partner in science class to work on a science project. However, you and your lab partner don't usually work together and can't seem to agree on a topic.

How would you work this out?

Hint: When you work together, you must ensure that you do something that benefits you both, but it's likely that both of you will have to sacrifice or amend your original idea.

39. What Are Your Intentions?

Your friend asks you to study together after school, but you tell them you can't make it, as the last time you hung out, she distracted you from your studies. The science test coming up is important, and you really need to concentrate.

Another friend, who is a top student in science, invites you over to their house, but when you get there, your other friend is already there.

She's upset and calls you out on this. You didn't upset her intentionally.

How would you handle this situation?

How could you explain your intentions to her?

40. Making Apologies

You're with a group of friends at lunch, and you say something unkind about one of your classmates without realizing they have just approached your group and are standing right behind you. They confront you.

What would you do?

How would you make amends for your actions?

Hint: Sometimes, we must apologize, especially if we're in the wrong.

41. Figuring Out the Intentions of Others

One of your friends has been distant lately, and you're not sure what's going on. After dinner, you call them, and it turns out they're at another friend's house. This friend has also been distant lately, and usually, you all hang out together.

At school the next day, you find out some other kids in your class were invited too, and you're not sure why you weren't invited.

You confront your friends, and they say they thought you'd been invited. You're not so sure.

How does this make you feel?

How can you figure out if this is an honest mistake or if they have done this on purpose?

42. Mediating

You usually hang out with two of your good friends. Recently, they've been arguing over who is the better soccer player because one got picked for the school soccer team while the other wasn't.

It's a pointless argument that achieves nothing, but now, you can't all sit together at lunch as the arguments are getting heated.

How could you help them resolve the conflict and become friends again?

43. Using Manners

The delivery man left a package at the neighbor's home while your family was away. You know it's for you, and you're excited, so you head over to the neighbor's house.

What would you say to your neighbor?

Hint: Think about politeness and how you would use your manners.

44. Dealing with a Fall-Out

You and your friend have had a disagreement and are not talking. They make it into school before you and sit with your friendship group. When you walk into class, they roll their eyes at you, but you really don't want to drag your other friends into it.

How could you try and understand your friend's point of view?

What would you do to try and end the conflict?

45. Being Supportive

Your friend didn't get the grades he'd hoped for in one of his classes, and he's upset. He said his parents are going to be even more disappointed than he is, and he's worried about showing them his report card.

How would you support your friend?

Is there anything he could do to improve his grade?

Personal Development

Personal development refers to the way you develop your own skills and understanding for personal growth. This means understanding your strengths, the limitations you face, as well as your ability to understand, accept, and deal with the actions of others.

46. Building Confidence and Courage

You're interested in playing for the school football team, and your teacher has invited you to practice. When you arrive, you see there's nobody there you know, and you feel like turning around and walking away.

How do you build up the courage to go and give it a go?

Remember, we all feel nervous from time to time, but we can't let it prevent us from doing the things we really want to do in life. Think of ways to overcome your nervousness.

47. Taking Responsibility

Your mom has assigned you some weekly chores to earn your allowance, as she said it's time you took on some responsibilities. You told your friend you'd walk to school with them and you're already running late. As you're leaving the house, you remember it's garbage day. You need to collect the garbage from the kitchen and pull the garbage bin into the street. It will make you even later than you already are, and you really want to meet your friend.

What should you do?

Hint: There are always consequences for our actions. Consider what the consequences will be if you don't take out the garbage.

48. Being a Good Listener

Your friend calls you and has something important to tell you, but you're a little distracted as your house is busy today.

How can you be there for your friend by being a good listener?

Hint: Active listening is the key here. Do you know what it means to actively listen?

49. Contributing

Your teacher is hosting a group discussion and said that everyone must contribute. You hate speaking out in class, as you're afraid you will get it wrong. You talk to your teacher, and they explain that this is about sharing opinions and ideas, so there are no wrong answers. You still feel nervous.

What would you do to ensure you do your part and contribute toward the project?

Hint: Sometimes, it's best to prepare by making notes.

50. Being a Team Player

You're in the last couple of seconds of a basketball game, and both your team and the opposing team have the same score. You dribble the ball down, and you really want to score the winning shot, but you're surrounded by three people who are taller than you and you can barely see the basket. You can see another team member, and they are in the perfect position to take the shot – all you have to do is pass.

You have two options:

a) You really want to score the winner, so you go for it and take the shot yourself.

b) You pass it on to your teammate.

What would you do and why?

Hint: Discuss the importance of teamwork.

51. Learning to Lose

You're in a robotics competition for your school. You and a student from another school make the final. There's a rivalry between your school and theirs, and throughout the competition, things have got a little heated.

You've enjoyed the competition overall, and they win by one vote. Of course, you're feeling disappointed.

How can you show good sportsmanship to the winner?

What positives can you take away from your experience?

Hint: Losing is a part of life, but it can be difficult. It's important to find ways to cope with this.

52. Making Difficult Decisions

You hang out in a friendship group of six, and four of you are in art class together. You have to complete a group project, but you can only work in a group of three. You've been assigned a group leader, so you have to pick two people to be in your group.

How would you decide who to pick?

How would you explain your decision to the person/people who you don't pick?

Hint: Remember, this is to complete schoolwork, so it's not about who you like the most. Some decisions you make in life have to be more objective.

53. Coping With Change

You're in a history class with several of your friends, but due to your good grades, your teacher wants to move you into the advanced class. You really enjoy the subject, and the move means you'll have more opportunities and could exceed your previous expectations regarding grades.

You have doubts because of some of the things you've heard: The lessons are more difficult, the teacher is really tough, you'll have to stay at school for an extra hour every Wednesday, and nobody you hang out with is in the advanced class.

How would you cope with this change?

54. Showing Gratitude

Last year, your grades started to slip in math. Your teacher has been super helpful, providing you with extra resources, asking another student to provide peer support when necessary, giving encouragement, and giving you extra credit work. After putting in hard work, you end the final semester with an A.

What helped you attain this grade, and how do you feel about those who helped you?

How could you express gratitude?

Hint: Gratitude can, of course, be shown to others but remember we can also feel gratitude for ourselves.

55. Disappointments

You've auditioned for the lead in the end-of-term theater performance, and you really want the part. A classmate who has previously bullied you gets the role instead, and you feel extremely disappointed. You got picked for a smaller part.

What would you say to the classmate who got the main part?

How could you embrace the part you were given positively?

56. Owning Your Mistakes

You're struggling with an essay, but you've been telling everyone it's going great. You're too embarrassed to ask for help. A classmate asks you to look over their essay and let them know what you think. It's really good, so you borrow some of their ideas to get you started.

Your teacher calls you both into her office. You usually do well in her class, so when she mentions that your essays were similar and asks what's going on, your classmate begins to cry. She explains she's going to have to call in both of your parents if she doesn't get to the bottom of it.

You know you must do the right thing, and honesty is the best policy, but how can you own this mistake?

57. Staying Focused

You've got important homework to do, but your brother is in and out of your room asking for help with his math homework, and your grandma has just reminded you that you haven't taken the dog out for a walk yet. Then your friend knocks at the door because she has some interesting gossip to share, but you're no further forward with your homework.

How would you handle this situation?

How can you ensure you get some time to focus on your important homework without any further distractions?

Hint: Prioritizing your time effectively is a key skill that can help you stay focused and motivated on what you have to do.

58. Taking Care of You

You've had a really challenging week. There's been drama between some of your friends, and you've had lots of homework. You've decided that this weekend, you're taking a break.

What could you do to take care of yourself?

What do you like to do to relax and unwind?

What do you like to do for fun or as a hobby?

59. Developing Confidence

You have to do a presentation as part of your class assessment. This means you must go to the front and tell your whole class about a book you've read, and you need to say why you like or dislike it.

Your presentation is tomorrow, and you're feeling really nervous.

What can you do to prepare for the presentation?

Whom can you ask for advice and support?

Hint: Think about ways you can practice to help build your confidence, and also how you can relax and calm your nerves.

60. Owning Up to a Lie

You're invited over to your friend's house for a sleepover. Your parents say you can go, provided you've done your chores and your homework. You tell your parents you've done both, but this isn't true. Although you've completed your chores, you haven' finished your homework, but you really want to go.

What would you do?

What would you say to your parents?

Made in the USA
Las Vegas, NV
04 February 2024

85317583R00085